I0748857

FINDING CHASITY

FINDING CHASITY

A Romance Novel

Uhn Muas

Vang Publishing House

ISBN: 979-8-9952834-3-0

Published by Vang Publishing House
Maplewood, Minnesota

Cover Design: Lexii Luther

Printed in the United States of America
First Edition

Dedication

To my children, you can do anything that you set your mind to.

Table of Contents

Xavier + Chasity's Playlist

"Lover" – Taylor Swift

"Golden" – Harry Styles

"Until I Found You" – Stephen Sanchez

"Electric Love" – BØRNS

"I Like Me Better" – Lauv

"Adore You" – Harry Styles

"Rewrite the Stars" – Zac Efron & Zendaya

"Perfect" – Ed Sheeran

"Say You Won't Let Go" – James Arthur

"You Are the Reason" – Calum Scott

"A Thousand Years" – Christina Perri

"Paper Rings" – Taylor Swift

"Yellow" – Coldplay

"Speechless" – Dan + Shay

"You and Me" – Lifehouse

Chapter 1

XAVIER

Nick pushed open my office door without knocking and strolled in like he owned the place. Judging by the relaxed grin on his face, he looked like a man with absolutely no responsibilities in the world.

"What are you up to?" he asked as he plopped down into one of the leather chairs in front of my desk.

Aimme, my executive assistant, rushed in behind him and nearly tripped over her own two feet. Her clipboard was clutched tightly against her chest, and she kept her eyes glued to the floor.

"I'm so sorry, Mr. Sterling," she said breathlessly. "I told him you were busy, but he insisted on coming in."

I waved my hand dismissively. "It's okay. He never listens anyway."

Aimme nodded quickly, grateful for the escape, and hurried out of the office. The door clicked softly shut behind her.

I leaned back in my chair and turned my attention back to Nick. Nick, or better known in the high society circle as Nicholas Warrington, was my best friend and business partner. Or more accurately, my silent partner.

Not because he preferred working behind the scenes, but because he had absolutely no interest in doing any real work. The man had more money than he knew what to do with. Even if he never lifted a finger to work for the rest of his life, he would still have billions leftover for the next ten generations sitting comfortably in his accounts.

Nick came from old money… very old money. His family privately owned Warrington Oil Industries, one of the largest oil companies in the country, and their wealth traced back almost as far as the Rockefellers. In addition to their oil company, their portfolio included prime real estate across several states, wealth management, and, more recently, investments in tech. New York, California, and Texas were just some of the major real estate holdings they owned.

Most of Nick's extended family did not work. They received enough income from their family trust that many of them were simply philanthropists. Except for Nick's parents, they chose to have a purpose in their lives.

By the time Nick turned eighteen, he was already part of the top 1% of the population. However, his family's trust fund had one small stipulation: even if a Warrington chose not to work and preferred to lounge for the rest of their life, they had to graduate from a four-year college in order to gain access to the trust fund.

That was the only reason why Nick went to college. And thankfully he did because that was how we met. Though I was genuinely surprised when he chose to continue onto graduate school. That had been completely on his own accord.

I, on the other hand, came from a middle-class family in Ohio. My father was a financial planner, and my mother was a stay-at-home mom. We lived in a quiet suburb where everyone knew everyone, and the biggest excitement most weeks was just the high school football game. Or whoever ran the red light at the main intersection in town.

Even after my father passed away from a stroke during my junior year of high school, we did not struggle financially. He made sure to plan his life insurance accordingly so that it was able to pay off the house and cover college tuition for both my sister and me.

My mother only had to pick up a very part-time job at the local library to manage utilities and groceries. Once we were old enough to work, my sister took a job at the local ice cream shop, and I worked at the fast-food joint. We made enough money to spend leisurely.

Nick and I met in an accounting course during our freshman year. It was by pure accident that we happened to sit next to each other on the first day of class. As we started talking, we found out that we had similar interests. One thing led to another, and Nick taught me how to invest in the stock market. He offered to loan me fifty thousand dollars to get me started on day trading. I had refused because it was a lot of money for me despite it being pocket change for him only.

I took out a personal loan for twenty thousand dollars and carefully analyzed the market. Once I learned what I was looking for, day trading got easier. Within six months, I paid back the personal loan. By the time I graduated with my bachelor's, I was able to retire my mother and have enough to continue into an MBA program. The very same one that Nick got into as well.

In graduate school, that's why Nick started teaching me about real estate investments. With the help of his family connections, I started building my real estate portfolio. One property at a time. By the time that we graduated, my portfolio had grown to be worth over a million dollars.

Then we launched our company, Sterling & Co. Originally, I wanted it to be Sterling & Warrington or Warrington & Sterling, but Nick had declined. He wanted to be in the shadows instead. We owned a chain of luxury resorts around the world. We started in the states then eventually spread throughout the world.

Our newest resort was going to be a luxury ski resort in Colorado. It was going to be our first winter resort. I already thought ahead that if it did well, we would expand to Utah next then maybe Alaska as well. Greenland was definitely on my list too.

Aside from our company, a side project that I had started was investments in new businesses. Without Nick, I would not have made it to where I was today. I may not have come from old money but through Nick's guidance and family connections, he helped me build my empire. So, I wanted to pay it forward. I backed many small businesses in New York. I was the silent partner behind them that laid the foundation for their business to stand on.

Not to brag but at least five of the newest and most popular high-end restaurants that recently received Michelin stars were backed by me.

I leaned back in my chair and crossed my arms. "What a pleasant surprise. I didn't even know you were back from Hawaii already."

"Been back," Nick shrugged with a grin. That immediately made me suspicious. In the years that I had known him, he was never one to cut his vacations short. Or even show up at the office as a matter of fact.

The man hated working so much that he did not even have his own office. Technically, we shared one, but it was more accurate to say that I worked at the desk while he lounged on the couch. Eventually I had to put both of our names on the door just to make it official. Whenever Nick did show up, he mostly drank from the bar in the corner and ordered Aimme around like a chicken with its head cut off.

"Well," I said, narrowing my eyes slightly. "What happened? Weren't you supposed to be in Hawaii for two weeks? It's only been one."

"Nothing happened yet," Nick said with a shrug. "We have that charity fundraiser tonight. I thought we could attend."

I stared at him then laughed. This was very suspicious indeed.

"You have not attended a single charity fundraiser in the last five years," I tapped my chin. "Besides, you told me that they were full of pretentious people only. They're boring. Everyone talks too much. That's why we just write a check."

Nick leaned forward suddenly; his expression suddenly turned serious. "I had an epiphany while in Hawaii."

"What are you talking about?" I muttered as a new email notification popped up on my screen. My attention turned to my computer screen and started reading the email. Swiftly, I typed a quick reply.

Nick pointed dramatically at me. "That! Right there! That's my epiphany! You work too much!"

He clapped his hands together. Now, he definitely was acting strange.

"Nick," I said slowly, "that's not an epiphany. You have been telling me that at least once every week since we started this company."

He shrugged. "Fine. Then it's time you start dating again."

I blinked.

"You haven't been in a serious relationship in… forever," he added.

I stood up and walked around my desk to stand in front of Nick. Gently, I placed the back of my hand against his forehead.

"Are you sick?" I asked. "Nicholas Warrington… the most notorious player in Manhattan… is encouraging me to date seriously?"

Nick shoved my hand away.

"Yes, I should be encouraging you to sleep around with all those actresses and models throwing themselves at you," he said.

"But I can't," he pointed at me. "I know you. You're a hopeless romantic."

He stood up and began pacing the office. I was sure that he was going to grab a drink from the bar in the corner, but he did not make a move in its direction. Very strange indeed.

"You want the house in the suburbs. The white picket fence. Two kids. Maybe a dog. You may be one of the most eligible bachelors in New York with billions in your bank account, but you're still the same guy I met freshman year."

He paused and his voice softened slightly as he looked at me.

"I've been watching you mope around for a year now. I really think it's time that you put yourself back out there, meet a nice girl, and settle down."

I leaned against my desk and shrugged. "Maybe dreams change."

"Whatever helps you sleep at night," Nick snorted. "Anyway, we're going to that charity fundraiser tonight whether you like it or not."

He rubbed his hands together and finally walked toward the bar.

"I saw a sneak peek of the list of bachelorettes," he added with a grin. "They're incredible. I'm planning to win a few."

He poured himself a glass of whiskey.

*****

Despite all my objections during the afternoon, here I was. Nick had practically dragged me here. If we did not have a public reputation to maintain, I probably would have been kicking and screaming the entire way.

The annual Westerly Foundation Charity Gala was being held in the ballroom of one of the most luxurious Manhattan hotels. The purpose of the fundraiser was to raise money for a network of privately owned hospitals that provided advanced medical treatments to patients living in poverty. Those privately owned hospitals obviously were owned by the Westerly Health System.

The medical treatments that were being offered for free were cancer treatments, medical surgeries, and life-saving procedures that people normally could not afford.

Nick insisted that we arrive early. Not because he cared about charity. No, it was because he wanted to inspect the bachelorettes before the auction started.

We each grabbed a glass of whiskey from the open bar and positioned ourselves near the entrance, where we had a clear view of the women being escorted into the back room. As Nick shamelessly ogled them, I rolled my eyes. If I rolled them any harder, they might pop out of my skull.

Most of the women were from influential New York families. Trust fund babies. Stuck up. Looking for a husband who could continue funding their lifestyles. Personally, that wasn't my preference.

I liked women who were down to earth and knew how much a bunch of bananas cost at the grocery store. Even though I personally have not been inside a grocery store in over a year. That's only because work kept me too late so Aimme took care of ordering all my groceries for me.

And besides, Nick had already slept with at least half of them. He was practically inviting chaos into his life. I did not envy it one bit. No siree.

"Hey guys," Bruce's voice startled us as he appeared behind us. "First time I've ever seen you two here… and early. Why are you two standing by the entrance like creeps?"

"Nick wanted to inspect the bachelorettes," I said as we shook hands. Nick barely glanced at Bruce before turning his attention back to the door.

"Where's Joe?" I asked.

Bruce squinted toward the stage.

"There," he said, pointing. His husband, Joseph Yang, was helping organize the bachelorettes backstage.

"You know how he is," Bruce said. "He insisted on helping coordinate everything."

Bruce Westerly was the only son of Katherine and Thayer Westerly, two legendary surgeons responsible for groundbreaking medical procedures in the field. Instead of following in their footsteps, Bruce built a billion-dollar tech company. Joseph, or Joe for short, was a brilliant cardiothoracic surgeon at one of their Manhattan hospitals. And the son that Bruce's parents had always wanted and eventually got.

"Isn't that Joe's cousin?" Nick suddenly asked. He pointed toward a petite woman with long black hair hurrying backstage. Bruce nodded.

"One of the bachelorettes broke her leg paragliding," he said. "Joe asked his cousin to fill in."

"Which cousin?" I asked.

Before Bruce could answer, the MC's voice boomed over the speakers welcoming guests to tonight's charity gala. Nick and I made our way toward our assigned table. His parents, Matthew and Nancy Warrington, were already seated there chatting with another couple.

I greeted them and took my seat. Events like this always make me uncomfortable. I still felt like an outsider among people who had grown up in this world. Nancy had practically trained me in etiquette over the years. If it were up to me, I'd be home in sweatpants watching Shark Tank with a pizza. But appearances mattered. Especially when you were in this tax bracket.

* * * * *

After introductions, a keynote speech, and presentations of the work that was being done by the foundation, the moment Nick had been waiting for finally arrived.

The bachelorette auction.

Nick bounced in his seat like a toddler promised ice cream. Slowly, the MC introduced one woman at a time. He read their introduction as they walked across the stage. Once they were at the center, the bidding began.

Nick quickly donated half a million dollars for a date with contestant number seven. She was a social media influencer with strawberry-blonde hair and sky-blue eyes. His ideal type. After she left the stage, another woman stepped out.

Time stopped.

The noise of the ballroom faded.

My breath caught in my throat.

It was her.

Chasity Yang.

Standing at five foot three, she somehow looked even more stunning than the last time I saw her.

Red lipstick outlined her perfect mouth.

Dark eyes that peered deep into my soul.

Long black hair cascading down her back.

Her black lace dress hugged every curve before flaring out mid-thigh and spread out on the ground around her. When I finally exhaled, I did not even know that I had been holding my breath. Nick looked over at me and grinned.

"You jerk," I muttered. "You knew she'd be here tonight."

He just nodded. I turned my attention back to the stage and realized that the bidding had already started.

"Four hundred thousand," I said as I raised my hand.

Chasity glanced in my direction. Our eyes met. I smiled. She quickly looked away.

"Four fifty!"

"Five hundred!"

The bidding began climbing rapidly. Nick leaned toward me.

"She's popular tonight," he said.

Then he pointed at my face.

"You're drooling."

I wiped my mouth quickly.

"Seven hundred!" I called out.

"Seven fifty!"

"Eight hundred!"

"Nine ninety-nine!" Nick shouted suddenly. I turned and glared at him. He shrugged innocently. I raised my hand again.

"One million dollars."

Chapter 2

CHASITY

I sat down in one of the chairs near the table and reached underneath it for my purse. My feet were killing me from dancing all night. I slipped off my heels with a sigh of relief and stuffed them into my purse before pulling out my trusty pair of Toms. It was a good thing I thought ahead and packed them. I had no idea how I would have survived the night if I had not brought them. After slipping them on, I leaned back in my chair and watched my cousins dancing on the crowded floor.

Music pulsed through the ballroom while laughter echoed between the crystal chandeliers. The room smelled faintly of champagne, perfume, and the sweet vanilla scent of the wedding cake that had been cut earlier in the evening. It had been so long since we were all together like this. Too bad not everyone made it to Joe's wedding.

I turned in my seat and slowly scanned the ballroom; I was curious to see who was still here enjoying the dancing and the open bar. Then my eyes landed on him. An angel of a man. I closed my eyes and shook my head. Nope. Impossible. No man could look that perfect. But when I opened my eyes again, he was still there.

Standing near the open bar, he was deep in conversation with another ridiculously attractive man. For a moment, I wondered if he might be gay. When a man looked that good, the chances were pretty high.

He was tall. If I had to guess, I would say that he was a little taller than six feet. Thick dark brown hair covered the top of his head. It had been styled just enough to look intentional without trying too hard. A faint five-o'clock shadow framed his jaw and made him look effortlessly rugged. His eyes were dark and intense.

And his tuxedo… Good Lord. It hugged his body like it had been custom-made just for him. I'm pretty sure that it was. He definitely looked rich enough to afford it. Maybe it was an Italian custom-made tux sourced right from Milan. Oh, how I crack myself up sometimes.

I caught myself staring at him with so much intensity that I quickly looked away. Hopefully, he did not notice me staring and thought that I was weird or creepy. Then my thoughts wandered back to him. I wondered what he looked like without any clothes on. How firm his chest might be if I leaned against it. Would his arms be so muscular beneath my fingertips?

Stop it! I mentally slapped myself. Joe had made me promise not to hook up with anyone at his wedding. Men like these did not date women like me seriously. These guys came from prestigious families with even more prestigious expectations. They fooled around with girls like me, then eventually married the rich daughters their families chose for them to strengthen business alliances.

I forced myself to turn my attention back to my cousins dancing and took a deep breath. Must focus on what was important right now. Celebrating Joe's happy marriage.

"Hi," the voice came from beside me.

I turned and nearly choked on my own saliva. The angel of a man was now standing next to me. How the FUCK did he get over here so fast? He was just by the bar a second ago.

"I'm Xavier," he said as he handed me a glass of champagne.

He was even more handsome up close. My stomach fluttered even more now than before. I could feel my entire body warmed up. Was it shyness? Or was I so severely attracted to him?

Oh, my goodness, down girl!

I reminded myself and tried to regain control of my thoughts. This had to be the alcohol thinking out loud. I normally do not drink this much, but tonight I indulged. I smiled politely.

"Chasity."

I took the glass from his hand and brushed our fingers. I felt a jolt of electricity run throughout my body and my eyes widened. I quickly drank half of the glass of champagne, one very unladylike gulp to cover up my sudden shock.

"So… how do you know Bruce and Joe?" I asked.

Xavier sat down in the chair next to me.

"Bruce and I met in college," he explained. "We've been friends ever since."

I tried to focus on his words, but I kept staring at his lips. They looked so soft, warm, and kissable. I wondered how they would feel against mine.

Danger! Danger! Danger!

I quickly shook the thought away. This man could still be gay. No need to disappoint myself any further.

My poor heart.

"That's cool," I said awkwardly.

"What do you do, Chasity?" he asked.

"I'm a psychologist," I replied after finishing the rest of my champagne and setting the glass down on the table. "What about you?"

"Businessman," he said, matter-of-factly, as he shrugged. He signaled for a waiter, who immediately brought us two fresh glasses of champagne.

After a moment, Xavier stood and held out his hand to me. "Would you like to dance?"

I drained the new glass of champagne. "Sure. Why not?"

The band switched to a slow song just as we reached the dance floor. Since I was now much shorter in my Toms, wrapping my arms around his neck wasn't exactly an option. Instead, I placed my hands lightly on his chest and left a few inches of space between us.

Apparently, Xavier wasn't a fan of personal space. His arms slid around my back and pulled me gently against him.

Well then. I thought; I was just trying to give him some personal space. As we continued to dance and drink throughout the night, we talked about everything and nothing at the same time.

He was originally from Ohio and moved to Manhattan after graduating from Harvard with an MBA. His family was living in

Albany, New York now. Spider-Man was his favorite superhero. And reading Harry Potter books was his guilty pleasure. But the most important discovery of the night? Xavier was *definitely* not gay.

During one of the slower songs, he wrapped his arms more tightly around me.

"Would you like to come back to my room with me?" he asked softly.

"Yeah," I said. The answer left my mouth before my brain could stop it. Oh no. Joe had warned me about this. Don't hook up with these men unless you're okay with it only being one night.

And honestly? I was okay with one night. One night with Xavier sounded pretty incredible to me right now.

We returned to the table so I could grab my purse. I slung it over my shoulder and quietly left the ballroom with him. Xavier placed his hand lightly on my lower back as he guided me toward the elevators in the main lobby area. Once inside the elevator and alone, he wrapped his arm around my shoulders and pulled me closer. I looked up at him as his dark eyes held mine. He gently tucked a loose strand of hair behind my ear before running the back of his fingers along my jaw. My lips parted slightly.

"I'm going to kiss you," he announced quietly. He did not ask if he could kiss me, simply told me that he was going to.

My heart pounded. Our lips were inches apart. I closed my eyes. Instead of crashing into me, his lips touched mine softly.

Slowly.

Carefully.

His tongue traced the edge of my lips. Electricity continued to be shot through my entire body. A soft moan escaped me, and he took the opportunity to deepen the kiss.

His hand slid to the back of my neck while his other arm wrapped around my waist to steady me. My fingers reached up and tangled in his thick hair. When he finally broke the kiss, he trailed his lips down my neck. A louder moan slipped out of my lips.

The elevator dinged breaking us from the moment. The doors opened and without another word, he grabbed my hand and led me quickly toward his suite. My short legs struggled to keep up with his strides. If his kisses were already this good, I wasn't sure how I would survive the rest of the night. But I guess I will find out one way or the other.

* * * * *

Morning came much too soon. I woke up slowly; heat was surrounding me. Why was it so hot? It wrapped around my body like a thick blanket; heavy yet comforting and pressed gently against my skin. The air felt dense as if the sun had crept in early just to linger a little longer with me. Warmth pooled on my back and curled around my shoulders. It seeped into my muscles until they loosened without effort. I could feel the softness beneath me and the quiet stillness of the room. There was a faint hum of morning beginning somewhere far away. Even my breathing felt slower and deeper. It was as though the heat itself was coaxing me to stay exactly where I was.

There was something peaceful about it. Something that made me not want to question it too much. The warmth carried a quiet kind of happiness. It was subtle but steady, like the feeling of being held without needing to be touched. It softened the edges of everything. My thoughts, worries, and even time itself until nothing felt urgent. My eyelids stayed heavy, not from exhaustion but from comfort. Opening my eyes might break whatever this moment was. I let myself sink into the gentle weight of the heat and the calm it brought.

Then I opened my eyes wide. Xavier.

The heat from him lingering against my skin as I shifted away. It was a quiet reminder of the night that we had just had. Suddenly, my bladder reminded me of its existence. Of course. The thought pulled a small, almost amused exhale from me as I carefully slipped out of bed. I was mindful of every movement that I made; I did not want to accidentally wake Xavier from his sleep. The floor was cool beneath my feet as I tiptoed into the bathroom.

When I came back out, the room felt the same. It was calm, untouched, and held onto that gentle hush that made everything feel suspended. I picked up my purse and checked my phone. The screen lit up my face in the dimness. There were no missed calls or text messages. A subtle sense of relief settled in my chest. No one needed to know that I had broken Joe's rule. The thought lingered, but it did not weigh heavy; instead, it folded into the moment, into the quiet satisfaction of everything being exactly as it was. Undisturbed, contained, and entirely my own.

It was only four in the morning. I still had a few hours before I needed to head back to my hotel and start sightseeing for the day. The thought settled over me gently like I had stolen extra time from the day before it even began. The room was quiet and wrapped in that early-morning stillness where everything felt paused and untouched. Outside, the world hadn't quite woken up yet. There were no loud noises or movement. Just a faint and distant hum that barely reached this space. I could feel the calm stretch of time ahead of me that was unhurried and still full of possibility.

Just as I slipped my phone back into my purse, it buzzed. The sound cut cleanly through the quiet and made my breath catch for a split second. A text from my sister. That was strange. She never woke up this early. It was only two in the morning in Montana.

Something in my chest tightened before I even opened it. A subtle shift from the ease that I had just been holding. My stomach dropped as I read the message. The words pulled me out of that soft and suspended moment into something heavier.

Dad had a stroke. We just rushed him to the hospital. No information yet but you should fly home ASAP. Just in case.

Just in case. The words echoed in my mind louder than they should be and heavier than anything else in the room. My heart nearly stopped. The air suddenly felt too thin and tight in my chest. The calm from moments ago shattered instantly and was replaced by a sharp and rising panic that spread through my body like cold water. Everything shifted and the warmth that had surrounded me just minutes ago was now gone. It left behind a hollow urgency that made it hard to think and breathe.

I turned toward Xavier. He was still asleep and looked peaceful. His chest rose and fell in a steady rhythm. For a brief second, I just stood there and watched him as the storm in my chest continued to build. Then reality pulled me forward. I quietly gathered my clothes with quick but careful movements. This was only supposed to be a one-night stand anyway. Without waking him, I slipped out of the room and headed back to mine. The door closed behind me with a quiet finality that felt far louder than it actually was.

Chapter 3

CHASITY

Why was this memory suddenly coming back to me? It had only been a one-night stand. An incredible one-night stand, I had to admit. The kind that lingered in ways I had not expected where it threaded quietly through the months without ever fully disappearing. It wasn't just physical closeness, but also it was the ease of how our time together felt effortless and consuming all at once. Ever since that night, no one else had even come close. And maybe that was the problem. Maybe I had measured every connection after him against something that had never been meant to last.

I sighed quietly; the sound was barely more than a breath. Leaving without saying goodbye had been intentional. A clean break. The kind that kept things simple. No expectations, complications, or chances of getting caught in something that would never choose me in the end.

A few days later, I had seen a picture of Xavier in the tabloids with a gorgeous woman draped on his arm. His girlfriend, according to the article. The image had settled something in me, something I had already known but did not want to admit. Joe was right. Men like Xavier did not end up with women like me. They married rich women who could strengthen business alliances and expand family fortunes. And women like me… we were just moments. Temporary, unforgettable maybe, but never chosen.

So why did he bid on me tonight?

"You were great out there, girl!" Joe's voice snapped me out of my thoughts as he high fived me enthusiastically.

"You snagged one million dollars for the foundation!" he continued excitedly. "That money is going to help so many people. Thank you so much for doing this for Bruce and me!"

I smiled. "No problem. I was here anyways, and I've never done anything like this before. It was fun."

Well… mostly fun. Except for the part where Xavier decided to bid on me. I still had no idea what he was thinking. When I was still on the stage, it had felt surreal where I was being bid on by so many millionaires and billionaires. But now that I was done with my part and back here again, it did not make sense why Xavier made the bid. Not with everything I thought I knew about men like him.

Unless he had simply been trying to support Bruce and Joe's family's foundation. That explanation felt safer and easier to hold onto. It turned the moment into something casual instead of something intentional. Although… it wasn't like other people hadn't been bidding. I remembered the voices and the rising numbers. All the energy that was filling the room. He had not needed to make any bids. There were plenty of other bachelorettes tonight. And yet, he did. The thought lingered longer than it should have, like a question that had never been answered and somehow still expected one.

"Come on," Joe said. "Let me introduce you to Xavier. He's one of Bruce's best friends."

My stomach tightened. As Joe led me toward the ballroom, the music grew louder with every step. It blended with the hum of voices and the occasional burst of laughter. The energy in the room was high and electric, and I noticed the next bachelorette was already going for over a million dollars. The numbers climbed with ease, as if they meant nothing. They were tossed around like casual conversation. It was shocking. And yet… not shocking at all. Rich people loved their charity tax write-offs. The realization settled in with a quiet cynicism and dulled the awe just enough to make everything feel a little more transactional. A little less glamorous.

After I left New York last year, I never told Joe about my one-night stand with Xavier. Or anyone else, for that matter. The memory had been mine to keep. I tucked it away neatly where no one could question it or complicate it.

Joe and Bruce had slipped out of their own wedding reception early to rest before their honeymoon flight the next morning. They left the night to unravel on its own. By then, most of the guests had been too drunk to notice that I disappeared shortly after midnight. No one questioned me about leaving early the next morning. Dad's stroke had been a perfectly valid excuse. And in a way, it had given me exactly what I needed. A clean exit and a reason that no one would challenge. It was the best way to leave everything that happened that night exactly where it belonged.

I sighed as we approached Xavier and Bruce's other best friend, Nick. I only knew Nick because he had helped me purchase my house. Well… technically, he helped me establish the trust since he had more free time than Bruce.

Why? That was a long story for another time.

As the distance between us started to close, my steps slowed just slightly. My mind was trying to remember the details that Joe had explained to me about the auction and dates earlier. From the looks of it, Xavier had already signed over the check. Right after someone won the bid, they quickly strode over to pay and claim their date details. It was clean, immediate, and had no hesitations. That was just the rules.

Because I had been a last-minute addition, the Westerly Foundation had made a special accommodation for me. Well… maybe it was also because I was Joe's cousin as well. The date was not going to be at any of the upscale restaurants like the others. Instead, it would be a simple day at the Central Park Zoo followed by lunch. Of course, everything was paid for by the foundation. I loved zoos and did not want to go through the hassle of having to buy two evening gowns. I already spent a little over two thousand dollars on the gown that I was wearing tonight. When I saw the price tag, I almost fainted. The sales associate told me that it was the cheapest dress that they had because it was from last season of Vera Wang's collection. And it was still over two thousand dollars.

The two men were standing near the donation table when we approached. They were deep in conversation and seemed completely at ease in a world that still felt slightly out of reach to me. The soft clink of glasses and low murmur of voices filled the space around them. It was polished and effortless. I forced my brightest smile even as something unsettled lingered beneath the surface. Nothing about this was complicated, I reminded myself. It was just a date. Just a donation. I was just helping Joe and Bruce out because a bachelorette had to drop out at the last minute. It was just another moment that would pass as quickly as it came.

"Hi, Chasity," Xavier said with a grin.

His smile melted me instantly. It was effortless, unguarded, and the kind of smile that did not just stay on his lips but reached his eyes and softened everything about him. It hit me before I could prepare for it. Before I could remind myself to stay composed. For a split second, I felt like I might actually dissolve on the spot, like the Wicked Witch of the West turning into a pathetic puddle at his feet. My breath caught, and my thoughts scattered in every direction. It was ridiculous how quickly he unraveled me without even trying.

This man was dangerous. Not physically, but emotionally. The kind of danger that did not leave visible scars but stayed with you long afterwards. It lingered in the quiet moments when you least expected it. Men like him did not fall… they simply entertained… they indulged… and then they moved on. And women like me… we were part of the experience but not the destination.

Technically, I wasn't poor, but compared to his world, I might as well have been. The difference wasn't just money. It was expectations, obligations, and legacies. When responsibility came calling and when real life demanded something more permanent… I already knew how that story ended. I would be the one left behind and hurt.

"Hi, Xavier. Long time no see," I responded calmly.

"You two know each other?" Joe asked as he looked between us surprised. We both nodded.

"Yes," Xavier said smoothly. "We met at your wedding."

Nick stepped forward and greeted me. "Hi again!"

I smiled at him and nodded. He seemed exactly like Xavier. There was an ease to the way that they carried themselves. A quiet assurance that came from never having to question where they belonged. Rich men with rich friends. The thought slipped in without any effort like something I had already accepted long ago.

Except Bruce. Bruce was genuinely kind. There was nothing calculated about him. I often wondered how he became friends with these two. These two were notorious for being photographed with models, actresses, and socialites.

Joe clapped his hands together, and the sharp sound cut through my thoughts pulling me back into the present moment. The energy around us shifted slightly, just enough to acknowledge him. I straightened instinctively with my smile still in place. My posture settled into something more composed. Whatever was about to happen next, I could feel the shift from observation to participation. From standing on the edge of their world to being pulled directly into it.

"Well, my job here is done. Babes, I must go help the other bachelorettes. I'll catch up with you later."

"No problem," I said with a smile. "Go do your thing."

Joe disappeared backstage.

"Well, I'm off to see if I can bid on a few more bachelorettes," Nick stretched dramatically and announced before clapping Xavier on the shoulder. "You kids have fun."

And just like that, he vanished into the crowd.

I let out a long sigh and headed toward the bar. I needed something to take the edge off the tension quietly building inside me. The closer I got, the louder the room seemed to become. I could hear the soft clinking of glass and the conversations people all around. Of course, Xavier followed as if it were the most natural thing in the world for him to fall into step beside me. One thing I learned about these charity events from Joe's stories was that there was always an open bar. It almost felt like a requirement. Liquid ease to match the polished atmosphere. Something to keep everyone's wallets open.

After downing two glasses of champagne, the warmth finally spread through me and loosened the tightness in my chest. Also, it dulled the sharper edges of my thoughts. The bubbles lingered on my tongue as I set the second empty glass down with a quiet exhale. I turned toward him.

"What are you trying to do?"

"Donate money to a good cause," he said casually.

I crossed my arms.

"Why did you bid on me? There were plenty of beautiful bachelorettes tonight."

He looked directly at me. "Because I like you."

His hand settled lightly on my lower back as he guided me toward one of the tables. The touch was subtle, but it sent a quiet awareness through me that I couldn't ignore. It wasn't possessive or forceful but just enough to direct and… to make his presence unmistakably close. The space between us felt smaller now as if the simple gesture had shifted something I had not been prepared to acknowledge.

Most of the people who had only come to make an appearance had already left. The ones remaining were either networking in focused conversations or continuing to bid on the auction. Their voices rose just enough to carry across the room before settling back into the steady hum. It felt more intimate now like the night had shed its polished surface and revealed what was beneath it all. And somehow, standing there with him, I felt more aware of everything. The room, the moment, and the quiet tension that seemed to linger just beneath the surface.

"Fine," I said as I sat down. "Meet me tomorrow at the Central Park Zoo at ten in the morning. We can look at the animals then grab lunch nearby."

Xavier leaned back in his chair and studied me.

"I like your choice for the date. I would have been more surprised if you had gone along with the cookie cutter dinner date at one of the upscale restaurants," he smiled slightly then changed the topic. "Your skin is glowing. And your hair looks shinier than the last time I saw you."

"I haven't noticed," I shrugged.

Small talk was dangerous territory. The more we talked, the easier it would be to fall for him. It was the kind of trap that did not feel like one until it was too late. From what I remembered last year, he was not arrogant like most wealthy men. There had been no condescension or disinterest masked as politeness. He had been present and attentive in our conversation. He asked questions about me. The kind that required actual listening and not just waiting for his turn to speak. And that, somehow, made him even more dangerous.

I felt it happening already. That quiet and subtle shift where curiosity could turn into something deeper if I let it. My guard tightened instinctively. It was a familiar defense that rose before I could talk myself out of it. Before he could continue, before he could ask anything else that might make me forget where I stood in all of this, I cut him off.

"It was nice seeing you again," I said quickly as I stood. "But I should go. It's late, and I'm exhausted."

I slipped into the back room to say goodbye to Joe. The shift from the crowded ballroom to the quieter space had an immediate and grounding effect on me. It felt easier to breathe and think back here. I kept it quick and simple. Nothing that would invite questions or delay me. Once I grabbed my backpack, I slung it over my shoulder. Without giving myself time to second-guess anything, I headed toward the hotel exit. The polished floors and dimmed lighting guided me out of a world that would never quite feel like mine.

There was still some light outside. The sky hovered in that in-between state where day had not fully given way to night yet. The air felt cooler and fresher. A sharp contrast to the warmth and closeness inside the hotel. Taking public transportation seemed safe enough, I thought to myself. I adjusted my grip on my bag and turned the corner. My mind was already shifting ahead to timing, routes, and distance when I collided with someone. The impact knocked the breath from me for a split second. My balance gave out. Before I could hit the ground, strong arms caught me and pulled me back into place. I looked up.

Xavier.

"What are you doing here?" I asked.

"Waiting for my date," he said with a smile. "I wanted to escort her safely home."

"No thank you," I said quickly. "I can get back just fine."

I tried to step away, but his arm remained around me.

Why did he have to be so strong?

I shook my head.

"I missed you," he said quietly. "It's been a year."

My heart skipped.

"Let me drive you home," he continued. "You'll save money."

I studied him carefully and let the moment stretch just long enough to think the decision through. He clearly was not going to give up. There was something steady in the way he stood there like he had already decided and was simply waiting for me to catch up. My eyes searched through his expression for any hesitations but found none. Queens was not exactly around the corner. The distance alone made me pause. My mind quickly ran through the practicalities of time and convenience.

Would it save time? Probably. The answer came easily, almost annoyingly so. Was I going to fall in love with him during a forty-minute car ride? Highly unlikely. The thought grounded me and pulled me back from the edge of overthinking. This did not have to mean anything. It did not have to become anything. It could just be a ride. Just a simple and practical decision. Yet, even as I told myself that, I hesitated for half a second longer than necessary. Some part of me knew that nothing about him had ever really felt simple.

"Fine," I finally muttered.

"See? That wasn't so hard," he said with a grin.

He grabbed my hand and led me toward the entrance where the valet parking attendant was. My short legs struggled to keep up with his long strides. *Just like late time,* my mind automatically went back to when he was leading me to the elevators.

The cool April wind hit our faces as we stepped outside. Without hesitation, Xavier slipped off his suit jacket and draped it over my shoulders. I glared at him, and he simply just smiled at me.

Why did he have to be such a gentleman?

A few minutes later, the valet pulled up with his car. A Tesla Model S. My eyes widened with my reaction being immediate and unfiltered. The car looked sleek even under the dim light. Its smooth lines caught just enough of the glow to make it stand out without trying too hard. It hummed quietly, which was a stark contrast to the usual rumble of engines I was used to. For a moment, I just stood there and took it all in. A small spark of excitement slipped through before I could stop it.

I had always wanted one. The thought came with a familiar mix of admiration and practicality. But the monthly payments were over a thousand dollars, and my reliable Toyota Corolla worked just fine. It always had. There was no fuss or unnecessary attention. It was simply just dependable and steady. Still, as I looked at the Tesla, I couldn't help but feel that brief pull of curiosity of how it might be like to sit behind the wheel.

Then my thoughts switched tracks… wasn't a Tesla for a billionaire a little modest? Shouldn't he be driving something like… an Aston Martin? I have no idea at this point. Xavier continued to surprise me. The valet opened my door, and I slid into the passenger seat.

"Where to?" Xavier asked. I showed him my address by angling my phone toward him so he could see it clearly. The glow from the screen briefly lit up the space between us before he nodded and entered it into the GPS with practiced ease. The navigation system chimed softly confirming the route as he pulled onto the road.

The city lights stretched ahead of us. Reflections slid across the windshield in long and fluid streaks. Everything inside the car felt smooth and quiet. I could not help myself and touched the sleek interior. My fingers brushed lightly over the smooth surfaces as if I needed to confirm it was real. The material was cool beneath my fingertips. I traced the edge of the console absentmindedly and took in the clean design. For a moment, I let myself just experience it.

"I see that you like my car," he said with a grin.

I rolled my eyes. "I love Tesla. I wanted one so badly, but the monthly payment is basically as much as a mortgage."

"Well," he said casually, "since you're here, you can ride in it as much as you want. If you're nice, I might even let you drive it."

"No thanks," I replied as I folded my hands in my lap. "I think it's better if we don't see each other after tomorrow."

He shrugged while keeping his eyes on the road.

"I guess. If you say so."

I know so.

Chapter 4

XAVIER

As I pulled up in front of Chasity's place, my stomach dropped. The shift was immediate. It was a quiet unease that settled in as the surroundings changed from polished city streets to something more worn and uncertain. This neighborhood was not in the worst part of Queens, but it definitely was not the safest either. The streetlights flickered unevenly along the block and casting long shadows across the cracked sidewalks. A few older cars lined the street. Their dull exteriors blended into the dimness, and somewhere down the block a dog barked behind a chain-link fence. It felt different here. It was much quieter but not in a comforting way.

I shifted the car into park, and the soft click sounded louder than it should have in the stillness. Then I turned toward her. The glow from the dashboard cast a faint light across her face.

"When did you get into town?" I asked.

She unbuckled her seatbelt and pushed open the door.

"About a week ago, I think," she said casually. "Well, thanks for the ride. I'll see you tomorrow at the zoo."

She stepped out of the car before I could say anything else.

"You're not going to invite me in?" I asked as I leaned across the middle console and gave her my best pathetic puppy-dog face.

Chasity was already halfway out of the car and moved with a kind of ease that made it clear she had already decided how this would end. She leaned back down toward the open window and flashed me that million-dollar smile of hers like nothing about this moment was complicated. For a second, it lingered before she shook her head slightly and closed the door. The soft thud felt final.

I laughed under my breath. The sound was quiet but certain. Oh no. I was not letting her escape that easily. The decision came naturally, without any hesitation. I quickly unbuckled my seatbelt and jumped out of the car. The cool night air wrapped around me as I jogged up the steps behind her. She was already unlocking the door with her keys in hand when she noticed me. The moment paused there.

"What are you doing?" she raised an eyebrow.

"I invited myself," I said with a grin.

Honestly, I just wanted to see where she lived. Curiosity, I told myself that it was nothing more than that.

Hopefully the inside looked better than the outside.

She rolled her eyes and that familiar hint of resistance flashed across her face. The door finally opened and she stepped inside. I followed without hesitation with the door closing softly behind me. The shift was immediately like stepping into a space that held its breath.

The house was small, but surprisingly well kept. The wooden floors creaked slightly under my shoes. Each step echoed just enough to remind me how empty it was. Something felt off about this house. The place was completely empty. There were no couches, chairs, or decorations. Just stacks of cardboard boxes scattered around the living room. Some were sealed; others were partially open like they had been searched through and abandoned mid-task. If this was an Airbnb, it was the strangest one I'd ever seen.

"Did you want something to drink?" she asked.

I turned around. And nearly forgot how to breathe. She had changed already.

Gone was the elegant dress from the gala. Now she wore an oversized T-shirt and a pair of soft pajama pants. Her long black hair was pulled back into a loose ponytail, and every trace of makeup had been washed from her face. She somehow looked even more beautiful now than just a few minutes earlier.

I finally realized my mouth was hanging open and quickly shut it.

"Uh… yeah. Coffee, if you have some. This is a cute little house," I said as I followed her into the kitchen and she placed a mug in front of me along with sugar and cream on the side.

"I know," she responded. "I fell in love with it the moment I saw it."

She looked around the room.

"It needs some TLC, but it's livable for now."

I blinked.

"Livable… for now?" I repeated slowly.

Did she just say what I thought she said? The words echoed in my head like I had heard them wrong or missed something in between. I glanced around again and took in the bare walls, scattered boxes, and the absence of furniture. Was she planning to stay here? The idea did not quite fit with everything I thought I knew about her or maybe everything I assumed. My gaze shifted back to her and searched in her expression to see if she was just messing with me. But nothing.

"That's enough chatting," she said quickly. "I'm tired and need to get to bed."

"Hey, I didn't even drink my coffee yet," I protested as she began pushing me toward the door.

She shrugged.

"That's your fault. I gave you ample time but you decided to talk and look around instead."

A moment later, I was standing outside her house with the door closed in my face. I couldn't help laughing. Once I got back into my car, I leaned my head against the headrest and sighed. She was completely different tonight than the woman I met a year ago. But to be fair… she had been drunk when we met. Still.

I had seen the way she looked at me earlier. The attraction was there. That much I knew for sure. And now I found her again. There was no way I was letting her slip away this time. I closed my eyes and let my mind drift back to that night.

After hours of incredible passion, she had fallen asleep in my arms. I had planned to take her to breakfast the next morning and see if she wanted to explore whatever had started between us. Truthfully, I had already decided I wanted more than just one night. When I woke up the next morning… She was gone. Completely gone. No note. No number. Nothing.

For a moment, I had considered demanding that the hotel staff give me her information. But that morning my mother called. My sister had gone into labor. Nick and I left immediately for Albany to be with my family. Later, I told Nick I needed to find her. He thought I should just let it go.

"If she felt the same way," he said, "she wouldn't have snuck out."

It had crushed me more than I wanted to admit. Chasity had been the first woman I truly liked since Amber. After that, I threw myself into work. I did not date. I did not bother looking. Until tonight.

I opened my eyes and looked back at the small house. A second chance. That's what this was. And I was not going to waste it. I was going to prove to Chasity that we belonged together. Just… not in a creepy way. That would be weird.

* * * * *

The ceiling in my bedroom looked brighter than usual that morning. For years I had always thought it looked dull and lifeless, but today something felt different. Life felt different.

I woke up in a good mood, something that hadn't happened in a long time. Usually, I had to drag myself out of bed, already bracing for another long day of meetings and paperwork. But today wasn't just another day.

Today I had a date with Chasity. A simple date. The zoo and lunch. Nothing extravagant. Still, it was better than nothing. A year ago, I had accepted the fact that I would probably never see her again. Yet here we were.

* * * * *

I spotted Chasity almost immediately when I entered Central Park Zoo. She stood near the entrance studying the zoo map on her phone. She wore an oversized sweater with a plaid scarf wrapped around her neck, tight dark blue jeans, and a knitted winter hat that covered most of her hair. The chilly spring wind tugged lightly at the ends of her scarf. She looked cozy. Comfortable. Beautiful. I quietly walked up behind her and wrapped my arms around her shoulders. She yelped and jumped out of my arms immediately.

"What the heck, Xavier!" she shouted, turning toward me. "You nearly gave me a heart attack!"

I laughed.

"Sorry," I said.

Then I grinned.

"But not really. It was kind of funny seeing you jump like that."

She shook her head.

"Whatever. That was not funny."

"Okay, okay," I said, raising my hands in surrender. "I'm sorry. I won't do it again."

She studied me for a moment before nodding.

"Anyway," she said, pointing toward the café near the entrance. "I was thinking we could grab coffee first. Then we can just walk around, look at the animals, people-watch… stuff like that."

I shrugged. "Sounds perfect."

We ordered our coffee at the café. I stuck with my usual: black coffee. Chasity ordered a vanilla latte. Before we started walking, she pulled up the zoo map on her phone and studied it carefully.

"Okay," she said, pointing at the screen. "We start at the Tropic Zone and then work our way around. The zoo is basically one big circle."

I nodded. Honestly, I had lived in Manhattan for nearly a decade and had never visited Central Park Zoo. Mostly because I never had a reason to. Until now.

Chasity started walking toward the Tropic Zone, and I quickly followed. For someone so short, she walked surprisingly fast. Without thinking, I reached for her hand and laced my fingers with hers. She stopped instantly. Slowly, she turned to look at me.

"What?" I said innocently. "We're on a date."

She looked conflicted for a moment. I could practically see the debate happening inside her head. Finally, she sighed.

"Fine… I guess."

As we wandered through the zoo, Chasity talked about her goal of visiting every zoo in the United States.

"The San Diego Zoo is still my favorite so far," she said as we paused near the penguin exhibit.

Listening to her talk made me smile. She spoke with genuine excitement, her eyes lighting up whenever she described something she loved. Just being near her felt… right.

Walking side by side. Talking about random things. Holding her hand. Now the only question was whether she felt the same way.

Nick had been convinced that I had only liked her because I was drunk that night at the wedding. But seeing her again now made everything clear. I remembered exactly why I had fallen for her so quickly. Chasity treated me like a normal person. Not a billionaire. Not a business opportunity. Just a man.

Our conversations flowed effortlessly, jumping from topic to topic. Movies. Travel. Psychology. Food. It did not matter what we talked about; she genuinely listened.

After about two hours of exploring the zoo, watching animals, and people-watching, we both agreed it was time to have lunch. Chasity led us to a small hole-in-the-wall sandwich shop a few blocks away. I was surprised she knew about it.

"I saw someone post about it on social media," she explained. "So, I looked it up. The locals say it's amazing."

Once we ordered, we found a small table near the window to wait for our food. Chasity studied the pictures hanging on the walls while I studied her. Finally, I broke the silence.

"Back to our conversation from last night," I said. "How long are you staying in New York?"

She shrugged. "I'm not sure yet."

Short answer. Her guard was back up.

A moment later our sandwiches arrived. I took a bite. My eyes widened. I stared at the sandwich in disbelief. I did not realize something this simple could taste this good.

"It's good, huh?" Chasity laughed.

I nodded slowly. I was honestly too busy enjoying the sandwich to form a proper response. We finished eating in comfortable silence.

Right as we finished, Chasity's phone beeped. She checked the message and smiled.

"I'm sorry," she said, standing up. "I must go. Thank you for bidding on me yesterday and for the date today."

She grabbed her bag. "I had a nice time."

I wiped my hands quickly with a napkin and stood. I wasn't letting her disappear again.

"Where are you headed?" I asked as I caught up with her. "You don't have a car. I can give you a ride."

She waved me off. "I'm meeting Joe and Bruce at a coffee shop. They sent me the address already. It's close enough to walk."

"In that case," I said casually, "I'll walk with you. Bruce is one of my best friends after all."

She sighed but did not argue.

*****

Three years earlier, Bruce had met Joe at that very same café. Joe had just moved to New York from Montana and started working as a cardiothoracic surgeon at one of the Westerly hospitals. Bruce had been so stunned by Joe that day that he completely forgot to ask for Joe's phone number. It was something that I had never let him live down.

For months, Bruce returned to that café, always ordered the same thing, always chose a seat with a clear view of the entrance, and hoped that Joe would walk through those doors again. I remembered the way he tried to act casually about it, like it was not a big deal. Even though it clearly was a big deal because he made me come with him on multiple occasions. Eventually, Bruce finally gave up. Or at least that's what he told himself.

Then one day, Bruce visited Westerly Hospital for lunch with his mother. And there was Joe. Just like that. No planning or effort. It was just chance stepping in where persistence had failed. The rest was history. And how did I know? I watched everything unfold with my own two eyes. If I was not with Nick, I was usually with Bruce. I orbited their lives in a way that felt natural back then. They were my only friends. Still the case today.

When we reached the café, we spotted them immediately through the window. Bruce and Joe were impossible to miss. Two impeccably dressed men. Bruce stood around six-foot-four while Joe was slightly shorter at five-foot-ten. Chasity waved enthusiastically as we walked inside.

"What do you guys want?" Joe asked when we joined them in the long line.

"I'll have the peach oolong tea," Chasity said after studying the menu.

"The usual," I told him.

Joe glanced around the café.

"Why don't you guys grab a table? I will order."

Bruce led us toward the back of the café and weaved through the narrow aisles with the kind of familiarity that came from returning to the same place over and over again. The soft hum of conversations and the clatter of cups created a steady backdrop that was warm and inviting. Their usual table was taken but we found another one nearby; it was close enough to still feel like part of their space. I slid into my seat. The worn wood of the chair was grounding in a way that felt oddly comforting, like I was stepping into a memory that hadn't quite faded.

When Joe returned with the cups of water for us while we waited for our drinks, he moved easily through the small space and balanced everything with practice ease. Joe had told me that he worked at a diner during medical school. It was the only place that allowed him to only pick up short shifts on the weekends. He set the cups of water down one by one, then his attention naturally shifted as he settled in. Joe turned to Chasity and his expression softening just slightly.

"Are you excited to start renovating your house?"

She shrugged. "More nervous than excited. I'm going to be watching a lot of YouTube tutorials."

I turned toward her.

"Oh… so that *is* your house," I said. "I was wondering why the Airbnb had no furniture."

Joe raised an eyebrow. "You went inside?"

I nodded.

"Yeah. I gave myself a tour. It's a little rundown, but nice. If you want, I can call one of my contractors. They mostly do commercial work, but I'm sure they could fit in a residential project."

Chasity immediately held up both hands.

"Whoa, slow down," she said. "I don't have any money right now. I spent all my savings buying that house."

She laughed softly. "Do you know how expensive houses in New York are?"

Just then Joe's name was called for the drinks. The barista's voice cut cleanly through the low hum of the café. He and Bruce stood almost at the same time and exchanged quick glances before heading toward the counter. Their absence left a small pocket of quiet at the table. Chasity and I sat quietly while we waited for them to return. The space between us filled with the soft clink of dishes and the faint hiss of the espresso machine in the background.

Inside my chest, excitement bubbled. It was impossible to ignore. She wasn't visiting. She had moved here. She was staying. The realization settled in and sent a quiet surge of anticipation through me. This was not temporary. This was not something that would pass in a few days and disappear. This was real. This was my chance. And I was not going to waste it.

Chapter 5

CHASITY

The lock on the door clicked behind me, and I leaned back against it. The sound settled into the quiet of the house like a marker that the day was finally over. I tilted my head up toward the ceiling and couldn't stop smiling. The feeling spread slowly and uncontrollably until it filled every part of me. Today's date with Xavier had been everything I imagined… and more. The memories replayed effortlessly in my mind. Each moment lingered just a little longer than it should have. My mind refused to let them fade too quickly.

He had shown up wearing a pair of dark jeans and a soft gray sweater that hugged his broad shoulders perfectly. It was an effortless style that did not need attention but drew it anyway. The casual look somehow made him even more attractive than the tuxedo he wore the night before. All the formality was stripped away and only left something that felt warmer and more real. There had been something disarming about it. Something that made the day feel less like an obligation and more like… something else. Something I wasn't quite ready to name.

And his smile…

Every time he smiled at me, my heart practically melted. Every time he touched me, even something as simple as holding my hand, my entire body lit up. It was like electricity ran through my veins. I craved his touch far more than I wanted to admit.

Our conversations flowed effortlessly. Just like they had the first night we met. It felt natural and easy. Like we had known each other for years instead of only sharing one night together.

He was just as kind and charming as I remembered. Maybe even more so. I groaned quietly and dragged my hands over my face.

"Ugh, I'm going crazy," I muttered to myself. I wanted that man so badly it was almost painful. Just my luck that the moment I moved to New York, I would run straight into Xavier again. Of course, avoiding him forever was never going to be possible. Bruce and Xavier had been best friends since college. That meant our paths were bound to cross sooner or later.

As perfect as Xavier seemed… I knew better. Men like him did not end up with women like me. Sure, we could have fun. We could flirt. Maybe I will even fall into another night of passion.

Eventually, reality would come crashing back in. He would return to his world of billionaires, boardrooms, and high-society expectations. I would return to mine. Two completely different corners of the world.

I pushed myself away from the door and slowly looked around the empty house. Calling it a house still felt strange. Back in Montana, my home was nearly three times this size. Yet somehow this tiny place in Queens had cost more than quadruple of what my old house had sold for. New York real estate was ridiculous. I shook my head.

When I sold my house in Montana, I sold most of my furniture too. It had been easier that way. Shipping everything across the country would have cost a fortune. In the end, I packed whatever I could fit into my little Corolla and drove to New York. Everything else stayed behind.

After arriving in the city, I left my car at Joe and Bruce's place. Parking in this neighborhood was already a nightmare, and my house did not have a garage yet. Another project to add to the ever-growing renovation list.

Stacks of boxes sat scattered around the living room. They were waiting to be unpacked. The faint smell of fresh paint still lingered in the air from the quick touch-ups I had done earlier in the week.

The place was far from perfect. The floors creaked. The kitchen needed updating. And the bathroom needed a new shower. But somehow… it already felt like home.

I walked slowly toward the kitchen and poured myself a glass of water. As I leaned against the counter, Xavier's face floated back into my mind again. The way he had looked at me today. The way his hand fits perfectly around mine. The way he smiled every time I started rambling about animals at the zoo.

My stomach fluttered.

Dangerous.

Very dangerous.

I shook my head and took a sip of water.

"Nope," I told myself firmly. "Don't even think about it."

Because if I let myself fall for Xavier Sterling… I had a feeling my heart would not survive the fallout at the end.

* * * * *

Someone was aggressively assaulting my doorbell. I groaned and rubbed my eyes. My body was still half-buried under my blanket as the sound cut sharply through the quiet. It wasn't just a simple ring. It was rapid and insistent, like whoever was on the other side had no intention of stopping anytime soon. The noise echoed through the house and bounced off the walls in a way that made it feel even louder than it actually was. My head throbbed faintly as I tried to orient myself. The lingering warmth of sleep slipped away far too quickly.

The ringing continued. Loud. Relentless. Each press of the bell was more impatient than the last. Like they were trying to make a demand rather than a request. I let out a slow and frustrated exhale. My hands dragged the blanket down just enough to glare in the general direction of the door. Even though I could not see it from where I was lying. Whoever it was, clearly was not going anywhere and ignoring them was not going to make it stop.

"Alright, alright…" I muttered.

I grabbed my phone from the nightstand and squinted at the screen. Seven in the morning. Seven.

This better be a life-or-death situation. Still half asleep, I threw on my robe and shuffled toward the front door. My feet dragged across the cold floor. When I opened it, a man in a construction vest smiled politely.

"Good morning, ma'am. We're here to start the renovation of your house."

I blinked at him. Then I shook my head. "Sorry… you must have the wrong house."

The man chuckled. "Nope. Mr. Sterling told us to be here bright and early. Some of my crew will help you pack up your belongings. We brought a storage pod to store everything in."

My brain slowly started waking up.

Oh. My. Goodness.

When Xavier said he could call a contractor, I did not realize he meant the renovation would start immediately. It had not even been twenty-four hours since we talked about it. Joe and I had not even reviewed any floor plans or designs yet. My Pinterest board still sat empty.

"Uh… okay," I said slowly. "I don't have a lot of stuff. Most of it is still in boxes anyway."

I stepped aside so the crew could enter. "Let me wash up first. Then I'll pack my bedroom."

The moment they walked in, I sprinted back to my room. My hands quickly grabbed a change of clothes, and then I rushed into the bathroom. While I waited for the water in the shower to warm up, I called Joe and put him on speaker.

"Hello?" he answered groggily.

"Dude," I said loudly over the running water. "Your friend already sent a contraction crew to my house!"

Joe laughed. "He moves fast. That's the businessman in him."

"Well, he could've warned me!"

"I'll get up and head over there," Joe said. "We can go over the floor plans and designs before they rebuild everything."

Then he hung up. I sighed, shook my head, and stepped into the shower. I was grateful for Xavier's help. But a warning would have been nice. So, I would not have to be showering while they were working on moving out my belongings to get ready for demolition. And why did they have to come at seven in the morning? I stayed up for half the night reading on my Kindle. Right now, I was basically a walking zombie.

After showering, I quickly packed my bathroom items into a duffel bag. Then I stuffed my clothes into two suitcases, deflated my air mattress, and shoved the bedding into another bag. My laptop and charger went into my backpack. Once I slipped on my tennis shoes, I started rolling the suitcases toward the door.

"Here, let me help."

I looked up.

Nick. He grabbed my suitcases and easily rolled them outside. That was unexpected. Joe always described him as the hands-off type. Maybe he was here to supervise the construction? Although, according to every gossip site on the internet and Joe, Nick preferred partying over working.

"Good morning, beautiful!" Xavier's voice drifted from the kitchen.

I groaned. Of course. Wherever Nick was, Xavier was not far behind.

Bruce had told me the two of them were practically inseparable in college. Xavier walked toward me and immediately wrapped me in a hug.

"Hmmm," he murmured. "You smell amazing."

He kissed the top of my head sending electricity from my scalp all the way down to my toes. *Damn it.* I did not think this feeling was going away anytime soon.

"Wow," I said loudly while trying to escape his arms. "Someone is coming on strong this morning."

He tightened his hold. "I'm not taking any chances on someone else winning you over."

I rolled my eyes. "Just help me carry these boxes."

I pointed at the stack on the floor.

"Yes ma'am," he let me go and stepped back to give me a mock salute. He stacked several boxes and carried them outside. Nick returned moments later to grab the rest. This renovation was clearly going to be intense. I let out a long breath.

* * * * *

"Guess who brought food!" Joe burst through the door holding a large brown bag in one hand and drink carrier in the other. He stopped abruptly.

"Oh my god," he gasped. "It looks like a tornado hit this place! They are fast and efficient!"

"I know," I laughed. "All my stuff is in the pod already. Apparently, the goal is to finish the renovation in a week."

Joe shrugged and handed me a coffee. "Who are we to stop them?"

He grinned.

"Let's have a picnic in the backyard while we go over floor plans, designs, and inspirations."

"Perfect."

We stepped outside, and I laid out a small picnic blanket on the small patch of grass so that we could sit on it without getting wet from the morning dew. While Joe unpacked the breakfast sandwiches from the bag, I glanced around to see if Xavier or Nick were nearby to offer them food. However, the both of them had mysteriously disappeared. Joe pulled out his phone.

"Let's start with your Pinterest board for inspirations first."

We scrolled through inspirational ideas, color palettes, and everything else that I never considered before.

"Look at all this potential!" he said excitedly.

"Oh," I said as my eyes lingered on a design. "White cabinets and black countertops for the kitchen."

The ideas grew quickly in my head.

"And maybe white, pink, and gold accents throughout the house."

I smiled. This turned out to be a lot of fun. I watched countless HGTV renovation shows in the past. Seeing demolition and design transformations always fascinated me. But doing it myself? That was a surreal feeling.

Within an hour, we had picked a color palette and started to make a list of the finishes that I wanted to take a look at. When I checked the time, my eyes widened. It was only ten in the morning. My day had started way too early.

"Are you guys done?" Xavier suddenly appeared behind us.

"Where did you and Nick disappear to?" I asked. "Joe brought breakfast."

I handed him the bag of sandwiches, and he took it. He shrugged casually as he reached into the bag to grab a sandwich. "We were supervising the renovation."

Then he glanced at the screen on my iPad.

"If you're finished looking at color palettes and ideas, why don't you guys head to the furniture showroom? The sooner we place orders, the faster everything arrives."

I turned and looked at Joe. "Are you free today?"

"It's my day off," he shrugged. "So, I'm free."

"I guess we're going furniture shopping," I said. After Xavier and Joe conversed about which showroom to go to, Joe and I headed out.

* * * * *

The moment we entered the showroom; a sales representative greeted us. His smile was immediate and polished. He gave off a feeling like he had been waiting for us specifically.

The space itself was bright and pristine. Furniture stretched across the floor. They were arranged by room. It felt different from the normal furniture that I had been to in the past. Definitely very different from Ikea. There were less people… Then I quickly glanced around. There were no other customers. My eyes went back to the furniture. Every piece looked like it was carefully curated and unique.

"Take your time looking around," he assured us. "Let me know if you guys have any questions."

Joe and I wandered through the space looking at each piece of furniture carefully. The room seemed to stretch farther than I expected. Each section flowing seamlessly into the next. Plush sofas, sleek dining tables, and carefully arranged displays filled the showroom. Everything was styled as if it belonged in a magazine rather than a store. The lighting was warm, intentional, and cast a soft glow over polished wood and textured fabrics. It felt less like shopping and more like stepping into different versions of someone else's life. Each setup was complete, effortless, and far removed from anything I had ever known.

One thing that confused me though was that none of the items had price tags. I slowed slightly, glanced from one piece to another, and searched for even the smallest label, but there was nothing. No numbers. No signs. Just perfection that was uninterrupted. How were people supposed to know how much they were spending? The thought unsettled me more than it should have. It was a quiet reminder that this was not a place built for people who needed to ask. Maybe they only told you at the register. Or maybe… if you had to ask, you were not meant to be here in the first place.

"This is the one!" I announced dramatically.

It was the tenth mattress I had tested. I sank into it slowly. The surface gave way just enough before supporting me completely. It was like it had been made specifically for my body. It felt like floating on a cloud. The mattress was soft, weightless, and the kind of comfort that made it hard to remember what anything else felt like. For a moment, I just lay there, stared up at the ceiling, and let myself enjoy it without overthinking.

Joe nodded to the salesman. The gesture was subtle but certain, like a decision had already been made. I pushed myself up slightly and glanced between the two of them.

"Now let's find you a bed frame," Joe guided me to more bedroom furniture.

I ran my hand along several beautiful headboards.

"These are all gorgeous," I said. "How am I supposed to choose?"

Joe laughed. "You picked a color palette, remember? White, pink, and gold. So, we just stay within that."

"When did you get so good at this?" I asked as I sat on a sectional couch.

"I've lived in New York for years," he shrugged.

I leaned my head against his shoulder.

"I missed you," I said softly.

"It was fun when everyone lived in the same town," Joe sighed. "I miss it too."

The sales associate followed us as we continued picking out furniture. Whatever the showroom did not carry; we decided to order online later.

* * * * *

"I guess I'll be staying at your place for a week," I said as we drove back to my house. The words came out lighter than I felt. The thought of not going back to an empty space and being surrounded by people sat somewhere between relief and uncertainty. The car moved smoothly through the streets. Sunlight slipped through the windows in soft flashes as we passed between buildings.

"We don't mind," Joe said warmly, his tone easy, like it was not even a question.

"Let's grab your stuff, then go get a late lunch. Bruce can meet us."

"Oh wow," I laughed as I shook my head slightly. "Mr. Bossy today."

Joe smirked. He was completely unbothered as if he had already decided how the rest of the day would go. Bruce was absolutely wrapped around his finger. The dynamic between them was effortless and almost amusing to watch. Joe made the plans, and Bruce happily fell in line. And somehow, without realizing it, I was already being pulled into that rhythm too.

* * * * *

When we returned to my house, the place was already in full demolition mode. A plumber was determining how to reroute pipes.

The kitchen had already been partially torn apart. An electrician worked on replacing and moving the old wiring.

"Did you guys have fun?" Xavier asked as we stepped inside.

Joe nodded. "We picked out most of the furniture. The rest we'll just order online."

"Ready for lunch?" Nick appeared suddenly. He flexed his arms dramatically showing off.

"I even helped remove the kitchen cabinets this morning. These muscles aren't just for decoration."

Xavier and Joe both shook their heads. Nick might be famous for his playboy reputation, but in person he was surprisingly goofy. The paparazzi never showed that side of him before.

"We were thinking of grabbing food near our place," Joe said.

"That works," Xavier shrugged. "Nick and I are staying at his house anyway."

"Perfect," Joe said. "I'll text Bruce."

I made my way to the storage pod and pulled the door open. I reached inside without hesitation. Everything was still where I had left it earlier before we left. I grabbed my backpack first then my suitcase. The familiar weight grounded me in a way that made everything feel a little more real.

With both in hand, I made my way back to the car. Joe opened the trunk with a soft click, and I loaded my things in before sliding into the passenger seat. The door shut quietly behind me and sealed me back into the calm interior. For a moment, I just sat there as the engine hummed to life.

Chapter 6

CHASITY

It had been a full week since the renovations started on my house. Between the start of my new job and settling into my routine in New York, I did not have time to stop by and check on the progress. I had been surviving on quick visits with Joe and Bruce in the evenings and crashing on their guest bed after long days at work. My days blended together in a steady rhythm of work, exhaustion, and just enough rest to do it all over again. The house had stayed somewhere in the back of my mind, something I had not quite let myself think about too much.

But today I finally had a moment to see it. As I pulled up in front of the house, my chest tightened and my eyes began to sting before I could even fully take it in. Tears filled my eyes and blurred the edges of everything as I sat there trying to process what I was seeing.

I could hardly believe the transformation. In just one week, the house looked completely different. The entire exterior had been repainted a soft and warm white which gave it a fresh and welcoming look that felt almost unfamiliar. The cracked walkway that used to lead to my front door had been repaired and lined with neat rows of flowers. Their colors were soft but intentional. Small garden lights had been installed between the plants. It was clearly meant to glow softly at night. It was like someone had thought about how this place would feel and not just how it would look.

It looked like something straight out of a home magazine. Perfect. Polished. Like it belonged to someone else. Then my eyes drifted to the side of the house. And there it was. My very own garage. I laughed quietly through my tears. The sound caught in my throat as relief, disbelief, and something deeper all tangled together at once. For the first time since everything started, it did not feel like I was just trying to catch up to my life. It felt like something had finally come together. Like this space and place was becoming mine in a way it had not been before.

Xavier had mentioned through Joe that they planned to finish the renovation today. My furniture was scheduled to arrive tomorrow morning. Only one more night of sleeping on an air mattress. Tomorrow I will finally have my real bed again. I grabbed the small box I had brought with me and walked toward the front door.

It was slightly open. I stepped inside and placed the box on the floor. When I looked up, my jaw practically dropped. If I had been a cartoon character, it would have hit the floor.

The living room fireplace had been completely redone. Fresh paint surrounded it, and a sleek sixty-five-inch television was mounted above it. On both sides were beautiful built-in shelves waiting to be filled with books and decorations. The entire room felt warm and elegant.

The kitchen had been moved from the middle of the house to the front, allowing sunlight to pour through the windows. White cabinets lined the walls, paired perfectly with smooth black countertops. A new stainless-steel oven and refrigerator gleamed under the lights. In the center of the kitchen sat a small island that was able to seat two people. It housed the microwave and additional cabinet space underneath. It was modern. Clean. Perfect.

I moved farther into the house and discovered a brand-new pantry and linen closet tucked neatly behind the kitchen. When I stepped into the bathroom, I froze. It was enormous. I had no idea how they managed to expand it this much within such a small house. The vanity stretched nearly five feet across the wall, giving me plenty of room for makeup, skincare products, and everything else I owned. There was a separate glass shower and a beautiful clawfoot bathtub sitting beside it. The toilet had its own sliding door for privacy. It felt like a spa.

I continued walking through the house in complete awe. Where my master bedroom used to be was now a dining room. A modern chandelier hung from the ceiling, casting soft light over a wooden dining table large enough to seat eight people. Eight people. I wasn't even sure if I knew eight people in New York yet.

To the left of the dining room were elegant French doors leading into the new master bedroom. I pushed them open slowly. The room was breathtaking. A beautiful chandelier hung from the center of the ceiling. On the left wall was a massive closet that stretched the entire length of the room. On the right side, a huge window overlooked the backyard, allowing sunlight to flood the space.

That's when I saw him. Six-foot-three inches of pure distraction. Xavier.

He was standing in the backyard wearing a black T-shirt and jeans. His shirt clung to him slightly from sweat, outlining the muscles in his arms and shoulders.

My breath caught. Down, girl. Down. Yes, he looked delicious. But he was off-limits.

I sighed quietly. Still… I wouldn't mind having a little fun. Before I could stop staring, Xavier looked up and noticed me watching him. He smiled and waved before walking toward the porch stairs that led up to the dining room.

A moment later he stepped inside.

"What do you think?" he asked with a grin, wiping sweat from his forehead.

I quickly wiped the corner of my mouth with the back of my hand. Hopefully he hadn't seen me drooling.

"It's even better than I imagined," I admitted.

He stepped closer and lightly tapped the tip of my nose with his finger.

"Have you seen the lower level yet?" he asked. "We didn't change much down there, but I think you'll like it."

I nodded quickly.

"I'll be outside," he added before heading back toward the yard.

I swallowed hard. Why was my body reacting like this? Maybe it had simply been too long. One year without sex was too long. That had to be the reason. Otherwise, I wouldn't be acting like some hormone-crazed teenager every time Xavier stood within ten feet of me.

Still… Who exactly was I supposed to sleep with? I did not know anyone in New York yet. And there were no convenient friends-with-benefits from Montana either. I sighed dramatically. How frustrating.

I walked down the stairs toward the basement to inspect the lower level. To the left were two newly finished bedrooms, each with large windows overlooking the backyard. To the right were the utility room and laundry area. When I opened the door to the garage, I smiled. It was spacious for a one-car garage. Shelves lined three walls, providing plenty of storage space. A heater hung from the ceiling clearly meant to keep the space warm during the winter.

I stepped back outside and headed to my car to grab my suitcases. All the items that had been stored in the pod earlier that week had already been moved back into the house. Time to start unpacking. I decided to start in my bedroom and work my way toward the front of the house, and eventually downstairs. It was finally starting to feel like home.

* * * * *

Fresh morning air filled my lungs as I took a deep breath through my nose, held it for five seconds, and slowly released it through my mouth. The warmth of the rising sun brushed gently against my skin. The weather was finally beginning to warm up and today felt like the perfect morning to do some yoga before starting the day.

My backyard had turned out beautifully after the renovations. Small trees lined the edges of the yard, and clusters of colorful flowers filled the garden beds. A soft breeze rustled through the leaves, carrying the faint scent of fresh soil and spring blossoms. If only the weather in New York stayed like this year-round.

I sighed happily. If it did, I would probably spend every morning out here.

The last few days had been a whirlwind of unpacking and organizing the house. Box after box had been opened, sorted, and finally put away. Anything I did not have, I ended up ordering online. Amazon quickly became my new best friend. Slowly, piece by piece, the house was starting to feel like home.

There was still one problem though. I needed to find an Asian grocery store. As much as I enjoyed ordering takeout, I missed cooking homemade food. Growing up, my mom had always cooked meals that filled the house with amazing smells: garlic, ginger, chili oil, and fresh herbs.

Now that she wasn't here to cook my favorite dishes for me, I would have to make them myself.

My thoughts shifted suddenly. Xavier never told me how much the renovations cost. I frowned slightly as I moved into another yoga pose. Surely it must have cost a fortune. The contractors had renovated my entire house in just one week.

One week.

Considering we were in one of the most expensive states in the country, the cost had to be well over one hundred thousand dollars. Maybe even more. Would the contractor let me set up a payment plan? I definitely need one.

Then another thought hit me. Wait… I did not remember giving my credit card to the furniture showroom either. I paused mid-stretch.

That was strange. I needed to ask Joe how much everything cost. Another item for my ever-growing to-do list.

I inhaled deeply again as I shifted into the next yoga position. And just like that, Xavier's face popped into my mind. That incredibly handsome man.

As a psychologist, I should technically understand why I couldn't stop thinking about him. But this felt like something science couldn't fully explain. Although… If I really dug through enough research journals, I might find something about the psychology of attraction and attachment.

Still. None of that would explain the way my stomach fluttered every time he smiled at me.

I sighed. Out of all the men I had dated before, not one of them compared to Xavier. He was different. Men in the past had been generous with gifts: flowers, dinners, expensive dates.

But Xavier was generous in a completely different way. He gave his time. His attention. His patience. The man had literally taken two weeks off work to help renovate my house and assemble furniture. Who did that?

Every time we spent time together, he spoiled me with sweet words and stories about his life. Through him, I caught small glimpses of the world he lived in, a world filled with billion-dollar companies, business deals, and powerful families. A world very different from mine.

He had been very open about his feelings too. Very open about wanting to pursue a relationship with me. And yet… I still wasn't sure how I felt about taking that step.

If he had been from a different tax bracket, I probably wouldn't have hesitated. But the difference between our worlds made everything more complicated. There were too many unknowns. Too many things that could go wrong. But then again…

Life itself was full of unknowns. We never truly knew what tomorrow might bring. Every day we took risks without even realizing it. Driving to work. Starting a new job. Moving across the country. So, what was life without taking risks?

My thoughts slowed. Was I really that afraid of falling in love with him?

When I thought about it honestly, every relationship carried risk. It did not matter whether the person was rich, poor, or somewhere in between. Relationships ended for all kinds of reasons. People fell out of love. People cheated. People changed.

Every relationship I was in in the past had all been a risk that I took with my heart too. Some relationships ended peacefully. Others ended in heartbreak. But I still took those chances.

Maybe a relationship with Xavier wouldn't be so terrible after all. At least I already knew the limitations. At least I knew what I was getting into.

My hands slowly came together in front of my chest. I bowed my head.

"Namaste."

Decision made. I was going to find out if Xavier was still interested in pursuing a relationship with me.

And this time… I wasn't going to run away.

Chapter 7

XAVIER

The sky outside my office window was bright, with only a few thin clouds drifting across the blue. It was the kind of day that made people want to leave work early. Unfortunately, I had a full schedule. Or at least I was supposed to.

I leaned back in my chair and stared out the window, completely unmotivated to do anything. It had been a few weeks since I last saw Chasity. After her house renovation was completed, after the furniture arrived and the landscaping was finished, I had stepped back.

She clearly hadn't liked how persistent I had been. So, I gave her space. But I was the one paying for it.

I miss her. More than I expected. More than I wanted to admit.

I sighed heavily and ran my hand through my hair. Who would have thought that I would become this pathetic over a woman? My heart felt restless, constantly wishing I could see her again. I never imagined I would turn into this kind of man. The kind who stared out the window thinking about a woman.

But here I was. Apparently, this was what it felt like when you found the one f. Another sigh escaped me.

"Mister Sterling, you have a call on line one," Aimme's voice crackled softly through the intercom.

"Thanks," I replied and picked up the phone. "Xavier Sterling speaking."

"Good morning, Mister Sterling."

The moment I heard the voice on the other end; my entire body froze.

Chasity.

Just minutes ago, I had been thinking about her. And now she was calling me. My heart jumped into my throat. I quickly sat up straight and pumped my fist in the air like a complete idiot. I couldn't believe she was the one reaching out first. I had been preparing myself to swallow my pride and call her.

"Good morning, Miss Yang," I said, trying to keep my voice calm. "What can I do for you this morning?"

"Well…" she hesitated slightly.

"I wanted to thank you for helping renovate my house."

A smile spread across my face.

"No need to thank me," I said casually. "I would have done that for anyone."

There was a brief pause on the other end of the line.

"Oh," she said slowly.

"Well… if that's the case, I guess I won't be inviting you over for a thank-you dinner tonight."

My heart nearly stopped. Did she just… Was she inviting me over? I sat up even straighter.

"If that's how you plan to thank me," I said quickly, "then I would very much like to be thanked."

I could practically hear the smile in her voice.

"I'll see you tonight at seven."

Then she hung up. I sat there for a moment, staring at the phone. Then I jumped to my feet and covered my mouth with my hand. My heart was racing like I had just won the lottery.

Chasity had invited me to dinner. At her house. Tonight.

I felt like a teenager who had just gotten his first date with the girl he'd been crushing on for years. I ran a hand over my face, trying to calm myself down.

Okay.

Focus.

I had work to finish. I sat back down at my desk and opened the first file. If I worked fast enough, I could leave early. Tonight was not a night I wanted to be late for.

* * * * *

"Hi!" Chasity greeted me when she opened the door. She was wearing a simple floral summer dress that swayed softly around her knees. Her face was completely make-up-free, and her hair was tied up in a high ponytail. The simplicity somehow made her even more beautiful. My heart skipped a beat.

"Hi, beautiful," I said, handing her the bouquet of flowers. I had stopped at a small floral shop on the way over. The florist recommended a mixed bouquet since I had no idea what Chasity's favorite flowers were. All I knew was that she liked flowers.

"You didn't have to," she said with a soft smile as she turned toward the kitchen to find a vase. I stepped inside and closed the door behind me.

"Everyone's out back on the deck," she said over her shoulder. The moment she said that my heart sank. Of course. It was too good to be true.

"Sounds good," I said as I headed toward the back porch. Joe, Bruce, and Nick were already sitting outside. Joe handed me a beer after I greeted everyone, and we made small talk while waiting for Chasity to come out. A few minutes later she appeared in the doorway.

"Since everyone's here, we can eat!"

Everyone moved into the dining room where the food had been laid out. Bruce and Joe slid into the built-in bench, while Chasity sat at the head of the table. I took the chair to her left, and Nick dropped into the seat beside me. Chasity clapped her hands lightly.

"I just want to thank everyone for coming tonight," she said. "Moving here was a big decision for me, and I'm really grateful to everyone who helped make it possible."

She turned towards me with a bright smile.

"And a special thank you to Xavier for finding the contractor so quickly."

"You still need to tell me how much that renovation cost," she added. "They worked incredibly fast."

"It was my pleasure," I said, smiling back at her.

"Don't worry about the contractor. I've taken care of it."

Nick dramatically leaned forward and sniffed the food.

"I didn't know you could cook!" he said, eyeing the dishes on the table. "This looks like Southeast Asian cuisine, right?"

"Yes!" Chasity said excitedly. "I was a little nervous cooking for you guys, but Joe said you've traveled all over the world."

Bruce grinned.

"Everything looks amazing."

"Dig in," Chasity said.

Everyone quickly began filling their plates. Dinner turned out to be incredible. The food was full of flavor, garlic, herbs, spices, and everything tasted homemade and comforting. After dinner, we migrated to the living room and sat around talking. Everyone shared their plans for the summer.

Chasity just started her new job teaching at Hunter College. Bruce and Joe were planning an anniversary trip to Alaska. Nick announced he was heading to Sweden with his "fling of the month."

As for me… I had no plans. Just work. Like always.

Eventually Joe stood up. "We should get going."

Bruce followed. Nick stood as well and gave me a quick wink. "I should head out too."

All three of them made their way toward the door. Chasity walked them out, saying goodbye before locking the door behind them. When she returned, she dropped onto the couch beside me.

"Well…"

I turned toward her and tucked one leg under me.

"Well," I repeated.

She smiled softly.

"Thank you for everything," she said.

"It was my pleasure."

I studied her face quietly. My heart was pounding so hard it felt like it might burst through my chest.

Her lips looked incredibly tempting. Soft. Full. It had been an entire year since I had kissed her. And I couldn't resist anymore. I leaned forward and gently kissed her.

To my surprise, she did not pull away. Instead, she placed her hand against my cheek. The kiss deepened slowly as she leaned closer to me. The moment stretched, warm and electric.

Then she suddenly whispered against my lips. "We shouldn't."

I pulled back slightly.

"Why not?" I asked softly.

She hesitated before answering. "First… Maggie Lancaster."

I froze.

"Maggie?" I repeated.

"Isn't she your girlfriend?"

I shifted so we were eye level.

"Is that what you're worried about?" I shook my head firmly.

"Margaret Lancaster is not my girlfriend. She never has been."

"Her father, Elliot Lancaster, is a business associate. He helped Nick and me with a few deals in the past. As a favor, I agreed to attend a few fundraisers with his daughter."

"That's all."

Chasity bit her lower lip.

"Well… that's not what TMZ said."

I sighed.

"TMZ is a gossip site. They'll write anything if it gets clicks."

In the past I never cared about what those articles said. But now… Now their gossip was sabotaging the one relationship I cared about.

"If you need more than my word," I added, "you can ask Bruce or Joe. Even Nick."

I paused.

"I'll even give you my mom's phone number."

Chasity nodded slowly.

"Okay."

I blinked. "Okay?"

"Yeah," a small smile appeared on her face and she shrugged. "I just wanted to see how you would react when I brought her up."

I stared at her in confusion. "You tested me?"

She laughed lightly. "I don't normally follow celebrity gossip, but I did Google you."

Of course she did.

"There wasn't much besides basic information," she continued. "But I saw a few TMZ articles about you and Maggie. I texted Joe and asked him about it."

"What did he say?" I asked carefully.

She smiled.

"He said Maggie is an annoying leech he can't stand."

I let out a long breath of relief. Thank goodness for Joe. Next time I saw him, I was getting him the most expensive bottle of wine from Nick's collection.

"So?" I asked.

Chasity stood up slowly and looked down at me.

"So…"

She crossed her arms and tilted her head.

"I think we should continue what you started a few minutes ago."

Chapter 8

XAVIER

When Chasity told me she wanted to go grocery shopping, I imagined it would be the kind of grocery shopping I occasionally did for myself. Which was always quick, efficient, and over within twenty minutes. In and out. Grab what you needed with no lingering and definitely not much thinking about the process since you already had a shopping list. I could not have been more wrong. From the moment we stepped into the first store, I realized this wasn't an errand. This was an event.

Chasity was doing the kind of grocery shopping that my mother did. The serious kind. The kind that required time, intention, and a level of knowledge that I did not even know existed. The first place we went was H Mart.

I quickly learned that H Mart was a chain of Korean supermarkets with locations all over the United States. The store was massive and filled with rows upon rows of items I could not name, nor did I know what they were used for. There were so many different colors and packaging that I had never seen before. I watched people move around quickly grabbing what they needed. They clearly knew exactly what they were looking for. Chasity moved through it all with ease. She picked things up, explained them to me, then occasionally tossed items into the cart without hesitation.

That was only the beginning. After H Mart, we went to two more grocery stores. Each one was just as intentional and added more to the growing pile of groceries in my trunk. Thank goodness I chose not to drive my Telsa today.

By the end of the trip, my arms were sore from carrying bags. The plastic dug into my fingers as we made multiple trips from the car. My mind was spinning from everything she had explained to me during our trip. The ingredients she bought, and the meals that she was planning to cook. Obviously, I had never cooked a day in my life except scrambled eggs and cup ramen, so all the combinations of ingredients were foreign to me.

Before today, I did not even know that any of these grocery stores existed. Yet as I watched her move through them so confidently, it was like second nature to her. Then she told me that she wanted to visit Chinatown next weekend for more shopping. I was already exhausted just thinking about it but I wouldn't miss it for the world.

"What are you making tonight?" I asked as Chasity moved around the kitchen, organizing ingredients and chopping vegetables.

"I'm making the Chasity version of pho," she said with a laugh. "I'm feeling Vietnamese tonight."

"Sounds good," I nodded. "The last time I had pho was at the Seoul airport."

Chasity paused mid-motion with the spoon hovering just above the pot as if time had briefly stalled. She turned to look at me slowly. Her expression shifted into something that landed somewhere between disbelief and mild amusement. Like what I just said was something completely ridiculous. One brow lifted slightly. Her lips parting just enough to respond before she stopped herself.

The kitchen felt quieter at that moment. The soft bubbling in the pot suddenly felt more noticeable against the silence. There was something almost playful in the way she looked at me. Like she was just… surprised. And maybe a little entertained.

"Why were you eating airport food?" she asked suspiciously. "Aren't you, like… rich or something? Don't rich people have private planes that serve fancy hors d'oeuvres?"

I burst out laughing. Did Chasity really think so highly of rich people? She was definitely a breath of fresh air.

"Not every rich person has their own private plane," I said. "I don't. I don't travel enough to justify one. When I do travel, I just fly first class."

She stared at me for a moment, dumbfounded.

"So, you only travel to your resorts?" she asked.

"Pretty much."

"You don't go on vacations?"

I shook my head. "Not really."

Chasity stopped what she was doing and turned to face me fully. Though her hands did not completely leave the task she was doing. One hand remained near the pot while her fingers were lightly gripping the spoon as she gave the broth a final stir before letting it rest against the side. Steam rose between us in curling waves that carried the deep and rich aroma of pho broth. Even as she shifted her attention to me, she still reached for the small container of MSG beside her and added it to the pot with practiced ease. Cooking and conversation existed in the same rhythm for her.

Her body angled toward me now, and her expression was amused. Then she let out a soft chuckle and slowly shook her head.

"You are the weirdest rich person I've ever met," she declared.

I raised an eyebrow. I was definitely *not* weird.

"I thought rich people loved traveling and showing off their money."

"Well," I shrugged, "firstly, I'm not a typical rich person. I still must work to earn money. Second, I don't exactly have a traveling partner."

She tilted her head. "What about Nick?"

"Nick travels like he's competing in some sort of international party Olympics," I said. "That's not really my thing. And Bruce is married now."

Chasity nodded thoughtfully as she returned to cooking. Her attention shifted back to the stove as if the conversation had simply folded into the rhythm of what she was doing. The soft sizzle of the pot filled the space followed by the steady and practiced sounds of movement.

I watched her for a moment longer than I meant to and took in the quiet focus on her face. She seemed completely at home in this space. The kitchen felt different now than the first time I came. It was warmer, fuller, and more alive in a different way. The scent of food began to build and wrapped around the room settling into the air.

"Wow," she said. "For someone rich, you have a very small circle. Technically only two friends."

I chuckled. "Thanks. That makes me sound sad."

"It's a little weird," she admitted. "But okay."

She dropped something into the pot and stirred. Her motions were slow and steady like she did not need to think about it. The spoon moved in quiet circles with the soft bubbling sound rising and falling as steam curled gently into the air. The scent grew richer with each pass. It was something warm and layered that filled the kitchen and settled deep. It was a feeling of comfort that I only felt when I went back home to see my mom. Chasity did not rush or break her rhythm. She just kept stirring like whatever she was about to say next could wait until the moment felt right.

For a second, she glanced up then back down again. I could see that she was organizing her thoughts in the same measured way she moved her hands. The light from above caught the side of her face and softened her expression. There was something calm about her presence. Like she was finally in a space where she felt relaxed.

"For the record, I love traveling. I try to go on a vacation at least once a year."

"Well," I said casually, "maybe we could go on a vacation together this year."

She snorted. "Fat chance."

"Why?" I leaned back in my chair.

"Because," she said, pointing a spoon at me, "I just spent all my savings on this house. And… I still owe you money."

"You don't owe me anything," I replied.

She gave me a skeptical look.

"You paid for the renovations and my furniture. That's not exactly nothing."

"If you really insist on paying me back," I said slowly, "we can arrange something."

She narrowed her eyes at me suspiciously. Her gaze sharpened just enough to make me feel like I was being examined rather than simply being looked at. It wasn't harsh, but it was deliberate. Like she was trying to read between my words and search for something I had not said out loud. The corners of her lips twitched slightly. It was not quite a smile but also was not quite serious either. She looked like she had not decided whether to challenge me or let it slide.

For a moment, neither of us spoke. The quiet simmer of the broth filled the space between us. Her eyes stayed on me. They were steady and unyielding making it clear to me that she was not convinced… at least not yet. She raised an eyebrow at me.

"Oh? What kind of arrangement?"

I stood up and walked around the kitchen island. Each step was slow and deliberate. The quiet of the space stretched just enough to make the moment feel heavier than it should have. The warmth from the stove grew stronger as I got closer. The scent of the broth wrapped around me. It was grounding and familiar.

She did not turn away from me but simply kept cooking like she did not notice what I was doing. Then I slipped my arms around her waist from behind and kissed the back of her head.

"Quid pro quo," I murmured near her ear.

She laughed.

"So, it *is* quid pro quo."

I kissed the side of her neck lightly. The contact was brief and gentle. My lips barely brushed her skin, just teasing her.

"Yes."

"And what exactly are your terms?" she asked.

"I want you to cook me dinner every night."

She laughed again.

"That's it?"

"That's it."

She thought about it for a moment. Her body went completely still in my arms like she was actually weighing her options. The pause stretched just long enough to make me second-guess myself. Her silence was deliberate, almost like she was teasing me. I could feel the shift in her breathing. The subtle change rose and fell as if she was holding back a reaction that she wasn't ready to show yet.

Then she smirked at me. The expression was slow and knowing, like she had already decided the outcome long before I made my move.

"I can do that," she responded. "But what if I get sick?"

"Then we renegotiate the terms," I shrugged.

Before she could react, I brushed my lips against her neck again. The action was a little less hesitant this time. I was purposely testing the edge of her patience. The moment barely landed before she twisted slightly in my arms. Her hand came up to swat at me. It was light and playful rather than serious.

"Stop doing that!" she said, half laughing. "Or we'll never get to eat dinner."

I stepped away quickly before I actually caused our food to be delayed and put just enough space between us to let her get back to the pot on the stove. A small smile lingered on my face; one I could not quite hold back even if I tried. The moment settled easily. It was a feeling that felt light and warm.

I watched her for a second. The way she moved with that quiet confidence in everything she did, and I felt something steady settle in my chest. I was so happy that I had her in my life. That I got to see her every day. It wasn't loud or overwhelming. I was just a quiet kind of happiness that felt real for the first time in a long time.

"I don't mind eating you instead," I teased as I kissed her cheek before retreating to the other side of the island.

I leaned back against the counter and watched her with an easy smile as she shook her head. She failed at trying to hide the hint of amusement on her face. The warmth of the moment lingered and settled comfortably into the space around us.

"Whatever," she said shaking her head, but she was smiling as she continued cooking. The corners of her lips gave her away. She tried to focus on the pot again and stirred with a little more intention than necessary. She was determined not to let me distract her any further. The soft clink of the spoon against the pot and the steady simmer of the broth continued to fill the space.

I stayed where I was and watched her without saying anything else. The teasing had settled into something quieter and comfortable now. The kitchen felt warm from the ease between us; the kind that did not need constant words to fill it.

Chapter 9

CHASITY

A few months ago, I was worried that moving to New York had been the wrong decision. Recently, however, I had finally started settling into a routine. From nine in the morning until about three in the afternoon, I was on campus. My days were filled with classes, office hours, meetings, and providing therapy at the college mental health clinic.

Afterward, it took about an hour for me to get home. Once I arrived, I usually meditated for a bit before starting dinner. Around six in the evening, Xavier would finish work and come over to eat. Some nights he stayed over. Other nights he went back home.

I sighed happily as I watched the neighborhood children playing in the front yards. This place was finally starting to feel like home.

"What are you looking at?" Xavier asked from the couch.

I turned away from the window and looked at the handsome man stretched out on my sectional.

"Just watching the neighbor kids play outside," I replied.

"Nick's parents are throwing their annual garden party this weekend," Xavier said casually. "I was wondering if you'd like to go with me."

I walked over and sat beside him. He slipped his hand into mine, intertwining our fingers.

"I'm assuming this isn't the kind of garden party where I can wear one of my summer dresses," I said. "I'll probably need to buy some designer dress, right?"

He nodded.

"Yes. Don't worry about it. I'll have Aimme book an appointment for you. And while you're at it, you should enjoy a spa day too."

"Wow, how generous," I said, kissing his cheek. "But I can pay for it."

He squeezed my hand. "I insist on pampering you. Please let me pamper you."

I laughed. "Fine. But for the record, I'm a gold digger. You've been warned. You can't complain later."

Xavier rolled his eyes.

* * * * *

The next day, Aimme called. She had everything planned out already. Of course she did. A dress appointment for Friday followed by a spa day for Saturday, then a hair and makeup appointment right before the party. Her voice had been bright and efficient, like this was just another event to coordinate and another detail to perfect. I barely had time to process it all before the plans were set in motion. My schedule was no longer entirely my own.

When I arrived at the building, I was not even sure that I had the right address. I slowed my steps and looked up at the structure in front of me, taking in the dark exterior. The building was painted black and dark blue. The colors blended together in a way that made it feel both striking and slightly intimidating. It looked like something out of *The Addams Family* or *The Nightmare Before Christmas*. It was dramatic and almost unreal compared to everything around it. For a second, I hesitated. I quickly pulled out my phone to check Aimme's text message again. Correct address. This was it.

Taking a deep breath, I stepped inside. The shift was immediate; the outside world fell away as the doors closed behind me. My chest tightened slightly from the weight of what this represented. This would be my first real glimpse into Xavier's world. And something told me… nothing about it would feel familiar.

"Welcome!" A woman greeted me warmly at the entrance. "You must be Chasity!"

"Yes, I am," I said as she motioned for me to follow her.

"I'm Raeann."

When we entered the next room, I froze. It was stunning. Crystal chandeliers hung from the ceiling and caught the light in soft and shimmering reflections that danced across the walls. Cream-colored couches sat elegantly around the room that were arranged with effortless precision. Every detail had been carefully considered. Mirrors lined the walls and stretched the space which made it feel even larger and more refined. It did not feel like a boutique. It felt like a luxury living room. It was private, intimate, and impossibly expensive.

"Please, have a seat," Raeann said.

I moved almost automatically and lowered myself onto one of the couches. The cushion was soft beneath me. It was supportive in a way that felt intentional. Another woman appeared as if on cue and placed a glass of champagne into my hand. The bubbles rose steadily and caught the light just like everything else in the room. I barely had time to process it before Raeann spoke again.

"You're even more beautiful than Xavier described," Raeann said thoughtfully. Her eyes scanned me with a level of focus that made me sit a little straighter. "I wasn't sure which dress would suit you, but now I know."

She disappeared briefly and left me alone in the quiet luxury of the room. The soft clink of my glass was the only sound as I set it down. A few moments later, she returned, and this time she wasn't alone. Two assistants followed behind her carefully pushing a rack lined with at least ten dresses. The fabrics alone caught my attention. There was silk, satin, and layers of delicate detail that seemed to shimmer even under the soft lighting.

"You're so gorgeous that you could wear any of these," she said enthusiastically.

"Well," I said as I tried to steady the sudden mix of excitement and nerves that I was feeling, "I guess I'll try them on and see which one I like."

I followed the assistants into the dressing room. The space was just as polished and thoughtfully designed as the rest of the boutique. They handed me dress after dress. Each one was more beautiful than the last. The fabrics felt different against my skin. Some were light and flowing. Others were structured and bold. Every time I stepped out and caught my reflection, it felt like I was looking at a different version of myself. The designs were stunning. Each one was carefully crafted. Each one capable of turning heads in their own way. Choosing just one felt impossible.

"Have you made a decision, dear?" Raeann asked.

I threw my arms into the air dramatically and let out a small, helpless laugh.

"I love all of them!" The words felt completely true. Each dress had its own kind of magic. Its own version of who I could be. For a moment, I just stood there. I was caught between too many good options. None of them were easy to let go.

After a long moment of thinking, I sighed. The decision was finally settled. "Maybe the dark blue one."

"That's an excellent choice," Raeann said without hesitation, as if she had been waiting for me to arrive at that exact conclusion. She quickly returned with a pair of heels and a set of jewelry. She held them up with practiced confidence. "Try it with these."

A few minutes later, I stepped out of the dressing room. The full look came together in a way that made me pause for just a second. The dress fit perfectly with the deep blue catching the light in a way that felt both elegant and effortless. The heels added just enough height. The jewelry was subtle but intentional. Everything balanced each other out and looked refined.

"You look magnificent!" Raeann exclaimed. Her voice was bright with approval. She turned to one of the assistants. "Wrap up this dress."

I quickly changed back into my regular clothes. It felt almost surreal, like I had just stepped out of someone else's life and back into my own. When they handed me the box, I hesitated, my hands hovering for just a second before taking it.

"How much do I owe you?" I asked nervously. The question came out quieter than I intended. I silently braced for the price.

Raeann waved her hand dismissively, like the answer did not matter. "It's already been taken care of."

I blinked. "Oh?"

"Xavier purchased everything you tried on today," she said casually. "Shoes and jewelry included. We'll have them delivered to your home later."

She laughed lightly, as if it were all perfectly normal. "I'm glad he finally found a woman to spend his money on."

I just stood there completely speechless. The words did not fully register at first. My mind needed a moment to catch up to what she had just said. I had only agreed to him paying for my spa day. Not ten dresses. Not… all of this.

"Thank you," I said weakly before leaving. The moment I got into my car, I called him.

"Hello, beautiful," he answered.

"Oh my god, Xavier. What did you do?"

He chuckled. "It wasn't that much."

"I just told Raeann I'd buy every dress you looked good in. You'll need them for events anyway."

"Xavier!" I protested. "Why would you do that? I was going to pay for it. I already owe you so much money."

"I swear it wasn't that expensive," he said.

"I have a work dinner tonight, so I won't come over. I'll pick you up tomorrow for the party."

Then he hung up. I stared at my phone. He hung up before I could argue with him. Ten dresses. Matching shoes. Matching jewelry.

This was overwhelming. I rubbed my temples. When I agreed to date him, I had imagined something simple. Romantic dinners. Flowers. Maybe a few gifts. Mind-blowing love making.

But in just a few months he had renovated my house, bought all my furniture, and now purchased an entire designer wardrobe. What was I supposed to get a man who could buy anything he wanted?

*****

"Wow," Xavier's jaw literally dropped when I opened the door the next evening.

I burst out laughing.

"Don't laugh," he said. "You're stunning."

He handed me a bouquet of flowers.

"Thank you," I said, placing them in a vase.

"Ready to go?"

"Yes."

I grabbed my wristlet and followed him outside. When we reached the car, he opened the back door. A driver. Of course. Apparently when attending a Warrington party, a driver was required. Xavier slid into the back seat beside me.

"You're very fancy tonight," I teased. He intertwined his fingers with mine.

"Just living up to rich people standards."

It took about an hour to reach Warrington estate. The property seemed endless. The drive from the main gate to the mansion alone took fifteen minutes. Lights illuminated the massive grounds and perfectly manicured gardens. My stomach twisted with nerves. This was my first official event with Xavier. I did not want to embarrass him.

"Took you two long enough," Nick said as he wrapped an arm around both of us when we entered the ballroom.

"It was getting boring waiting for you."

"It couldn't have been that boring," I said, looking around at the crowded ballroom. "There are plenty of women here."

"Not at these parties," Nick said. "Everyone's on their best behavior."

"Xavier!" We turned to see an older couple approaching. Nick leaned down and whispered in my ear.

"My annoying parents. Nancy and Matthew."

"Good to know," I whispered back. Nancy immediately hugged Xavier.

"It's so good to see you!"

Matthew shook his hand.

"And who is this lovely young woman?"

Nick released my shoulder.

"This is my girlfriend, Chasity," Xavier said.

Nancy hugged me warmly. "Welcome! I can't remember the last time Xavier brought a woman to one of our parties."

Matthew shook my hand. "Xavier is like a second son to us."

After greeting more guests, they moved on.

"I thought this was a garden party," I whispered to Xavier. "Why are we inside a ballroom?"

He shrugged. "I stopped questioning these things years ago."

We spent the next hour greeting other guests. Eventually the faces blurred together. Then suddenly…

"Xavier!" A shriek pierced the room. Maggie Lancaster. She rushed over and grabbed Xavier's arm. "When did you get back into town?"

Xavier gently removed her hand. "I've been here a while."

He wrapped an arm around my waist.

"This is my girlfriend, Chasity."

I offered my hand. "Nice to meet you."

"I didn't know you were into Asian girls," she said flatly and stared at me coldly.

Nick laughed.

"Why wouldn't he be? He owns resorts all over Southeast Asia."

He looked Maggie up and down.

"The last white girl he dated was completely insane."

"You bastard!" Maggie snapped.

"If the shoe fits," Nick said calmly.

She stormed off. We stepped onto the balcony afterward.

"Wow," I said.

Nick nodded.

"I know."

"She seemed so nice on social media," I said.

"Social media isn't real life," Xavier said softly, kissing the top of my head.

"You never have to worry about her."

I laughed. "I think you're the one worrying."

"I think dinner's about to start." Nick glanced toward the ballroom.

We returned to the ballroom and took our seats. Nick's parents gave their annual speech about supporting pediatric cancer research. Dinner was served. Course after course. Finally, the band started playing. Guests moved toward the dance floor. Then suddenly a woman stopped beside our table.

"Well, well, well," she looked directly at Xavier.

"Isn't this the man who left me at the altar?"

I stared at her in shock.

Nick groaned.

"Oh great. Her."

"Who is she?" I whispered.

Xavier sighed. "My ex."

"And yes. He did leave her at the altar," Nick added bluntly,

My eyes widened.

"Ten years ago," Nick explained.

"And she's still mad about it?"

"She likes playing the victim," Xavier said calmly. He stood and held out his hand to me. "But that's ancient history. Right now, I just want to dance with you."

Chapter 10

CHASITY

I placed my hand in Xavier's and let him guide me toward the dance floor. The band was playing a slow jazz song. Couples swayed gently under the warm glow of the chandeliers while servers slipped quietly between guests carrying trays of champagne. Xavier placed one hand on my waist and pulled me close. His other hand held mine as we began moving with the music.

"You okay?" he asked quietly.

"I think so," I replied. I glanced back toward the table where the woman had been standing earlier.

"Your ex seems… intense."

Xavier chuckled softly. "That's one way to describe her."

"You left her at the altar," I said, still slightly stunned. "That's a pretty dramatic story."

He sighed. "It was the right decision."

His voice was calm, but I could feel tension in his shoulders.

"Were you scared?" I asked.

"Of marriage?" he asked.

"No," I said. "Of hurting someone."

Xavier looked down at me for a moment.

"I wasn't scared of hurting her," he said honestly. "I was scared of marrying the wrong person."

His hand tightened slightly around mine.

"I knew it would destroy both of us in the long run."

I studied his face carefully. I felt warmth spread through my chest. We continued dancing quietly for a moment. Around us, people laughed, chatted, and moved across the dance floor in elegant circles. But somehow it felt like the room had faded away.

"You handled Maggie well," Xavier said after a moment.

"I did?" I asked.

"You didn't punch her."

"I considered it."

He laughed. "That would have been entertaining."

"I didn't want to embarrass you," I admitted.

Xavier stopped dancing for a second and gently lifted my chin so I would look at him. "You could never embarrass me."

His voice was soft but certain. My heart skipped.

"You're the best thing that's happened to me in a long time," he added.

I felt my cheeks warm. "You're laying it on pretty thick tonight."

"I'm just telling the truth."

The band transitioned into another slow song. Xavier pulled me closer.

"You know," he said thoughtfully, "when I first saw you again at that charity auction, I thought my brain was playing tricks on me."

"Why?"

"Because I had convinced myself I would never see you again."

My chest tightened.

"I didn't think you would want to see me again," I admitted quietly.

He frowned slightly.

"Why would you think that?"

"Because I disappeared after that night," I said.

Xavier looked surprised. "I thought you left because you regretted it."

"I left because my dad had a stroke," I said softly.

His expression immediately changed. "You never told me that."

"I didn't have your number," I said with a small shrug. "And when I saw you in the news with Maggie a few days later… I figured it was better to just move on."

Xavier shook his head. "That was the worst week of my life."

"Really?"

"I woke up, you were gone, and I had no way to find you," he gave me a small smile. "I even asked Nick to help track you down."

"You did not."

"I did."

"What happened?"

"He said it would make me look like a psycho billionaire."

I burst out laughing. "That sounds exactly like something Nick would say."

"But somehow you still found your way back into my life," Xavier smiled.

"New York is a big city," I said.

"And yet here we are," his thumb brushed lightly against my hand. "Do you regret it?"

"Regret what?" I asked.

"Giving me a chance."

I looked into his eyes. For a moment I saw something there I hadn't noticed before. Vulnerability. Real vulnerability.

I shook my head slowly. "No."

The band finished the song. The crowd applauded lightly. Xavier leaned closer to me.

"Good," he whispered. "Because I'm not letting you disappear again."

My heart fluttered. "I wasn't planning to."

Nick suddenly appeared beside us holding two champagne glasses.

"Wow," he said dramatically. "You two look disgustingly happy."

Xavier rolled his eyes. "What do you want, Nick?"

Nick handed us each a glass.

"To the future," he said with a mischievous grin. "And hopefully fewer crazy ex-girlfriends showing up at family events."

I laughed and raised my glass. "To that."

* * * * *

The cool marble of the restroom floor echoed softly beneath my heels as I stepped back into the hallway. The quiet of the corridor was a stark contrast to the lively sounds drifting from the ballroom. Laughter, music, and the clinking of glasses floated through the open doors like a warm wave pulling me back inside.

As I walked toward the entrance, the faint scent of roses and expensive perfume lingered in the air. Someone must have refreshed the flower arrangements while I was gone.

When I stepped into the ballroom again, the soft glow of the chandeliers immediately caught my eye. The room shimmered with gold light reflecting off crystal glasses and polished silverware. The band played a smooth jazz melody, the saxophone drifting lazily through the air while couples swayed across the dance floor.

My eyes instinctively searched the room. And then I found him. Xavier stood near the bar with Nick, talking to a small group of businessmen. His back was partially turned toward me, one hand casually resting in the pocket of his tailored suit pants while the other held a glass of whiskey.

God, he looked good. The dark navy suit fit him perfectly, the fabric hugging his broad shoulders and narrow waist like it had been made specifically for him. His crisp white shirt contrasted beautifully against the darker tones of the room, and the subtle silver watch on his wrist glinted under the chandelier light whenever he moved.

But it wasn't the suit that caught my attention. It was the way he carried himself. Confident. Calm. Effortless. He leaned slightly toward the men he was speaking with, nodding thoughtfully as one of them talked. Every now and then, he smiled or chuckled softly at something Nick said.

The deep sound of his laughter drifted across the room to where I stood. Even from here, I could hear it. Warm. Easy. Real. My chest tightened. It was strange seeing him like this. Among these powerful businessmen, dressed in luxury clothes, discussing deals and investments like he belonged at the center of it all.

Because to me, Xavier was still the same man who stood barefoot in my kitchen eating pho while teasing me about cooking dinner every night. The same man who wrapped his arms around me while I chopped vegetables. The same man who fell asleep on my couch while we watched movies together. The sweet boy next door who just happened to be a billionaire.

I leaned lightly against the wall, watching him for a moment longer. A server passed by with a tray of champagne, and the faint smell of citrus and sparkling wine mixed with the rich aroma of the dinner that had just been served, garlic, butter, roasted herbs. My mouth still carried the faint taste of the dessert we had just eaten, something sweet and chocolatey that melted on my tongue.

Somehow none of it mattered because my attention kept drifting back to him. Xavier lifted his glass and took a sip of whiskey, the amber liquid catching the light before disappearing between his lips.

I suddenly remembered the first time I kissed him. The taste of whiskey and mint on his breath. The warmth of his hands on my waist. The way my heart had nearly burst out of my chest. I swallowed slowly. What was happening to me?

I had promised myself when I started dating him that this would stay simple. Fun. Carefree. But the longer I watched him standing there, laughing with Nick, running a hand through his hair as he listened to someone speak, the more I felt something shift inside my chest. Something deeper. Something heavier. Something dangerous.

I exhaled quietly. I fell in love with him. The realization hit me so suddenly that my fingers curled slightly against the wall beside me. This wasn't just attraction anymore.

It wasn't just chemistry or excitement or curiosity. It was the way he looked at me when he thought I wasn't paying attention. The way he showed up every evening just to eat dinner with me. The way he kissed my forehead when he thought I was asleep.

My heart beat a little faster. And somehow that terrified me. Because loving someone like Xavier meant stepping into a world I had never belonged to. A world of garden parties, private drivers, designer dresses, and powerful families. A world where mistakes were magnified and gossip traveled faster than truth. Yet somehow, when he looked at me… None of that seemed to matter.

Across the room, Xavier suddenly laughed again and turned slightly. His eyes scanned the crowd. Then they landed on me. The moment he saw me, his entire face softened. His smile changed. Not the polite smile he gave to businessmen. Not the charming smile he used with strangers. But the real one. The one meant only for me.

Xavier excused himself from the group and began walking toward me. My heart fluttered. With every step he took, the sounds of the ballroom seemed to fade into the background until all I could hear was the quiet rhythm of my own heartbeat. When he finally reached me, he gently slipped his hand into mine. His palm was warm against my skin.

"What are you doing over here by yourself?" he asked softly.

I smiled at him. "Just watching you."

"Oh?" his eyebrow lifted slightly.

"Yeah," I said. "I was thinking…"

"What were you thinking about?" he asked.

"Just how strange it is that the man talking business with half the billionaires in this room…" I hesitated for a moment then shrugged lightly. I squeezed his hand. "…is still the same sweet guy who steals food off my plate at dinner."

Xavier laughed quietly.

"Well," he said, leaning down closer to me. "I have to keep your expectations realistic somehow."

My chest warmed. And for the first time since arriving at the party… I stopped worrying about whether I belonged in this world. Because standing beside him… It felt like I already did.

Chapter 11

XAVIER

"Mister Sterling, your twelve o'clock appointment is here," Aimme said through the intercom.

I nodded even though she couldn't see me. "Please send them in."

I leaned back in my chair and glanced at the clock on the wall before looking down at the reports spread across my desk. The steady hum of Manhattan traffic filtered faintly through the floor-to-ceiling windows behind me.

A moment later, my office door opened. I looked up.

Amber.

She stood in the doorway like she owned the room. Her long strawberry-blonde hair cascaded over one shoulder in soft waves, and the fitted charcoal dress she wore hugged every curve of her body. Her heels clicked sharply against the polished floor as she walked toward my desk, each step deliberate.

Amber swayed her hips slightly as she approached, the same confident walk that used to make heads turn wherever she went. Some things never changed. She sat down in one of the chairs across from me, crossing her legs slowly.

Amber Lancaster knew exactly how beautiful she was. For most of her life, men had worshipped the ground she walked on. Even now, at thirty-four, she was still stunning enough to stop traffic. But none of that mattered to me anymore.

Amber broke my heart ten years ago. And nothing would ever make me love her again. Not if hell froze over. Not if she were the last woman on earth. I would rather become a eunuch. She studied me for a moment, her blue eyes scanning my face as if trying to read my thoughts.

"Well," she said finally, a small smile forming on her lips. "That's quite the welcome."

I closed the file in front of me and folded my hands on the desk. "What are you doing here, Amber?"

Her smile widened slightly. "No hello? No 'how have you been?'"

"No," I said flatly.

She sighed dramatically and leaned back in the chair.

"I'm in town for a few weeks," she said casually. "Business, charity events, social obligations. You know how it is."

I did not respond.

Amber tapped one manicured finger against the armrest.

"I ran into you at the Warrington party the other night," she continued. "But you disappeared before we could really talk."

"That was intentional."

She laughed softly. "You always were brutally honest."

"I've learned it saves time."

Amber tilted her head slightly, studying me again.

"So," she said slowly, "the rumors are true."

"What rumors?"

"That you finally settled down."

My jaw tightened slightly. "If you're referring to Chasity, then yes."

Amber's expression flickered for a brief second before she masked it with another smile.

"She's cute," she said. Something in her tone made my stomach tighten.

"She's more than that," I replied calmly.

Amber leaned forward slightly. "You're serious about her."

It wasn't a question.

"Yes."

The word hung in the air between us. Amber studied my face for another long moment. Then she laughed softly and shook her head.

"I never thought I'd see the day."

"What day?"

"The day Xavier Sterling falls in love again."

The room suddenly felt very quiet. I did not respond. Amber leaned back again, crossing her arms.

"So, tell me," she said. "What makes her so special?"

I looked at her directly in the eyes. "Everything."

Amber went silent. For the first time since she walked into my office, she did not seem amused. She seemed thoughtful. Then she slowly smiled again.

"Well," she said as she stood up. "I guess that answers my question."

She walked toward the door, then paused with her hand on the handle.

"Oh, Xavier?"

"Yes?"

She glanced over her shoulder.

"You might want to hold onto her." Her smile turned slightly mischievous. "Women like that don't come around very often."

Then she opened the door and left. The moment it closed behind her; I leaned back in my chair and exhaled slowly. Amber Lancaster had never visited my office before. Not once in ten years. Which meant one thing. She hadn't come here to reminisce. She had come here for a reason. And I had a feeling that reason had something to do with Chasity.

* * * * *

Nick and I were eating lunch outside that day after one of our classes. The weather was warm, and the sky stretched above us in a perfect shade of blue without a single cloud in sight. Students filled the courtyard, their voices blending with the distant sound of music from someone's speaker.

I was halfway through a sandwich when Amber walked by. She had a backpack slung casually over her shoulder while the two girls beside her carried small crossbody bags. Amber wore a pink tank top and light blue skinny jeans, the sunlight catching the soft golden tones in her strawberry-blonde hair.

She was laughing about something her friend had said. The sound of her laughter drifted across the courtyard. And just like that… My heart was gone. She was the most beautiful woman I had ever seen.

Later that afternoon, Nick told me who she was. Amber Lancaster. Her father had once been a mayor, and her mother came from the Rockefeller family. Old money. Influence. Power.

Everything I wasn't. I knew right away that I did not stand a chance with someone like her. I was just a middle-class kid trying to build a future for myself.

Which was why I was so shocked when she noticed me. I was even more shocked when we started dating. For the next four years, I loved Amber with everything I had.

One of my favorite memories was the weekend when we flew to Paris. Nick had loaned me his family's private jet so I could surprise her. We spent the weekend wandering the city, eating pastries in quiet cafés, walking along the Seine, and visiting museums.

On the final night, I took her to dinner at a five-star restaurant overlooking the Eiffel Tower. After dinner, we strolled through the glowing streets of Paris. The Eiffel Tower sparkled against the night sky, thousands of lights twinkling like stars. That was when I dropped to one knee. I asked Amber to spend the rest of her life with me.

I had secretly flown both our families and our closest friends to Paris to witness the moment. A photographer hid nearby to capture the proposal. Amber cried when she said yes. I thought I was the luckiest man alive.

Her parents hosted an extravagant engagement party when we returned. Nearly every major family in high society attended. Amber spent the next year planning the wedding of her dreams. We scheduled it for one month after graduation. Everything seemed perfect. Or at least I thought it was.

The day of the wedding arrived. I sat in the groom's room at the church with my groomsmen, laughing and talking about the upcoming football season. Then suddenly…

The door slammed open. Nick rushed inside, breathing hard. His face was pale and sweat dampened his hairline. Everyone turned to look at him.

"Where have you been?" one of my groomsmen asked. "And why do you look like that?"

Nick shook his head. "Xavier… please don't shoot the messenger."

The way he said it made my stomach tighten.

"What happened?" I asked.

Nick stared directly into my eyes. "Your sister showed me something. I think you need to see it before you say I do."

My chest tightened. "What did my sister find?"

Nick swallowed. "She went to the restroom earlier. When she came back, Amber and the bridesmaids were talking."

He hesitated then blurted it out. "Amber hooked up with Marshall last night."

The room exploded with shocked voices.

"Marshall?" one of my groomsmen said in disbelief. "That drug dealer?"

I leaned back in my chair and covered my face with my hands.

"Are you sure she wasn't just messing with you?" I asked quietly.

Nick shoved his phone toward me. "Look."

"This is her social media. Do you even follow her on social media?"

"I don't have any social media accounts," I muttered. "It's useless to me."

But I took the phone anyway. As I scrolled through the photos, my stomach slowly dropped. Picture after picture. Dates. Locations. Weekend trips she had told me about were girls' getaways. Except Marshall was in every single one.

My hands began to shake. The picture from last night was still there. Amber and Marshall. Together. Everything suddenly made sense. How could I have been so stupid?

Nick grabbed the phone back and opened a video. "Watch this."

The room fell silent as the video played. Amber sat with her bridesmaids, laughing.

"I'm only marrying Xavier because he can give me a secure future," she said casually.

One of her friends spoke up. "But he's such a nice guy."

"He's not my type. He's a good boy." Amber rolled her eyes and laughed. "He's boring. Always talking about his business plans with Nick."

Then she smirked. "Marshall is different. He's a bad boy. Everything with him is exciting."

Her friends giggled.

"With Xavier," Amber continued, "I get to be the trophy wife. I can go on vacations whenever I want with whoever I want."

She shrugged. "He probably wouldn't even notice. Win-win."

Her friends burst out laughing.

Nick stopped the video. The room was completely silent. I stood slowly and walked toward the window. My chest felt tight. Like something heavy had been placed on it. For four years…

I had loved this woman with everything I had. She was supposed to be my future. My wife. The mother of my children. We were going to buy a house. I wanted to have two kids. Maybe a dog too. Live happily ever after. But none of it had been real.

Nick stepped beside me and placed a hand on my shoulder. "I'm sorry, Xavier."

"Don't be," I took a deep breath. At least I knew the truth. "I'm glad you found out before I ruined my life with someone who never loved me."

My groomsmen gathered around me.

"What do you want to do?" one of them asked.

I exhaled slowly. "Tell my mom and sister that the wedding is off. There won't be a wedding today."

The words felt heavy, leaving my mouth. But they also felt right. Then I looked at the group of men surrounding me.

"If you guys are still up for it…" I gave a small smile. "I have a presidential suite reserved in the Bahamas for a week. We could fly down there and party."

Nick slapped my shoulder and grinned. "That's my man. Don't let her bring you down. She's not worth it."

He already had his phone out. "I'll call my pilot."

One by one, my groomsmen nodded. Without another word, we walked out of the room. Out of the church. Out of the wedding. And straight toward the Bahamas.

Chapter 12

CHASITY

"Ready?" Xavier turned and smiled at me. He grabbed both of my hands and gave them a reassuring squeeze before bringing them to his lips and kissing them gently. I took a deep breath, held it for a moment, and slowly let it out.

Why was I so nervous? It wasn't like I had never had a boyfriend before. There had been a handful of boyfriends in my past, and I had met many of their parents. Parents usually liked me. I was harmless to their sons. I had never felt this anxious meeting with someone's family before. But for some reason, meeting Xavier's mother had my heart racing.

I kept taking deep breaths, trying to calm myself. Oh god… what if his mom was snotty like Maggie or Amber? What if she looked at me and decided I wasn't good enough for her son? I knew Xavier and I lived in different worlds. I had already accepted that our relationship probably wouldn't last forever. But I did not expect the end to come soon.

Would she offer me money to leave him? Like in those ridiculous dramas? Okay. I needed to stop. I was getting way ahead of myself.

"It'll be okay," Xavier said softly. He leaned across the center console and kissed my temple. "My mom will love you."

He glanced at the house and then back at me. "Come on. We've been sitting in the car for fifteen minutes. My mom, my sister, my brother-in-law, and my niece are waiting to meet you."

I couldn't trust my voice, so I just nodded. Here went nothing. We stepped out of the car and walked toward the house. Before we even reached the porch, the front door flew open.

A beautiful older woman stood in the doorway.

"Xavier!" she exclaimed, smiling brightly as she opened her arms. She wrapped him in a warm hug before turning to me with the same enthusiasm. "And you must be Chasity!"

Before I could react, she pulled me into a hug as well.

"It's nice to meet you, Mrs. Sterling," I said once she released me.

She laughed softly. "Darling, Mrs. Sterling was my mother. Just call me Mom."

Then she linked her arm through mine. "Come inside. Brunch is ready!"

After everyone greeted each other, we moved out to the patio to eat. The backyard was peaceful and cozy, with a small garden and a wooden swing under a large tree. Plates of pancakes, eggs, fruit, and pastries filled the table.

"So," Penelope said, leaning forward and pointing her fork between Xavier and me. "How did you two meet?"

Xavier glanced at me. "Would you like me to tell the story?"

I smiled. "Sure. I want to hear your version."

"Well," he began, "we first met at Joe and Bruce's wedding last year. Chasity was one of the bridesmaids. The moment I saw her walking down the aisle, I just knew."

He looked at me and smiled softly. I rolled my eyes playfully.

"After dinner I tracked her down," he continued. "We danced, talked, and got to know each other. Then we lost contact. A few months ago, Nick and I attended a charity fundraiser, and Chasity happened to be there. We reconnected. And here we are."

Penelope smiled warmly. "That's adorable. I'm glad you two found each other again."

The conversation shifted to Lily's upcoming birthday. Penelope and Joshua discussed party plans while Lily proudly described the decorations she wanted.

After brunch, Penelope decided to take a nap. Pregnancy had left her constantly tired. Xavier and Joshua took Lily to the nearby playground while debating which football teams would make it to the Super Bowl this season.

Mrs. Sterling guided me into the living room with two cups of tea. She placed her hand gently over mine.

"Chasity," she said kindly, "Xavier told me you've been hesitant about getting serious and meeting the family."

My stomach tightened.

"He's my son, so of course I'll say good things about him," she continued. "But his heart was broken once. Very badly. That's why he closed himself off from dating. You're the first woman in ten years that he's shown any interest in."

She looked at me gently. "Please give him a chance to prove himself to you."

I hesitated before answering.

"It's not that I don't want to give him a chance," I said carefully. "We just come from very different worlds. I could never live up to the expectations of high society… or what people might expect from Xavier's wife. I've watched my cousin struggle for years trying to fit into that world."

Mrs. Sterling suddenly laughed. "My dear girl, we don't run in that circle."

"You don't?" I blinked in surprise.

"No," she said warmly. "I shop at Target and buy my clothes at Old Navy. My parents were poor farmers. I only graduated from high school. Xavier's father's parents were farmers too. His father was the first in the family to go to college."

She shook her head. "I've never attended any of those high-society events. Xavier only goes because of the empire he built with Nick."

"Oh," I said quietly, surprised. "I thought… since Xavier is a billionaire… you were all socialites."

"No," she said firmly. "And I don't expect you to follow any of their ridiculous rules either. Too many restrictions for my taste."

I looked down at my hands. "I just didn't want to embarrass him."

"Xavier didn't come from money either," Mrs. Sterling squeezed my hand gently. "All I'm asking is that you give him the chance to show you how much he cares."

I nodded slowly. “Okay. I can do that.”

She smiled warmly and began pulling out photo albums. For the next hour she showed me pictures of Xavier growing up. Xavier looked exactly like his father. His father had been incredibly handsome.

Mrs. Sterling laughed as she told stories about how girls in their town fought over who could date Mr. Sterling. Then she shared stories about Xavier as a young boy and how his life changed after meeting Nick.

“Chasity!” Xavier’s voice echoed through the house.

“We’re in the living room!” Mrs. Sterling called back.

Xavier peeked inside. “Ready to head out?”

I nodded. We said our goodbyes and promised to visit again soon. Lily clung to Xavier’s leg, begging him not to leave until Joshua finally lifted her away from her favorite uncle. Soon we were back on the road heading toward my house.

“That wasn’t so bad, was it?” Xavier asked.

“No,” I said with a smile. “I really like your family. Your mom is so sweet.”

I lifted his hand and kissed it.

“Well,” Xavier said, smiling at me, “I can’t wait to meet your family.”

I laughed. “We can visit them. But I can’t promise they’ll be as welcoming as your mom. My parents are very traditional.”

Xavier shrugged confidently. “Don’t worry. I’ll win them over.”

* * * * *

“Mom, we’ll be landing at four, so just have Justin pick us up from the airport,” I told her over the phone. She had been calling me every day since I told my parents I was coming home to visit. No matter how many times I confirmed our landing time, she kept asking again. It had been two months since I met Xavier’s family, so it was about time he met mine. If I was serious about this relationship, I needed to start putting in more effort.

“But which airline are you flying?” Mom asked immediately. “Please tell me you’re not flying United. Remember that doctor they dragged off the airplane?”

I laughed. “Mom, that was a one-time incident. And it was years ago. But no, we’re not flying United.”

“Okay,” she said, sounding relieved. “I’ll see you tomorrow.”

Then she hung up. No matter how old I got, my mom would always be overprotective.

I was the oldest of three children. My younger sister Alexi was the middle child. She was married to a wonderful man my parents adored. Alexi worked as a nurse, and my brother-in-law Stephan was a banker. They had two kids. The oldest, Betty, was five and was starting kindergarten in the fall. The younger one, Josiah, was three and already as bossy as toddlers could be.

My younger brother Justin was the youngest. He was currently in a serious relationship and had already told my parents he planned to propose by the end of the year. Out of all of us, Justin was the most business minded. He ran his own graphic design company and worked as a photographer on the side. His girlfriend, soon to be fiancée, was an elementary school teacher.

When I first decided to move to New York, my parents weren't thrilled. They would have preferred that I stay in Montana. But they eventually understood why I wanted to go. Joe even flew out to Montana personally just to reassure them that he would look out for me.

"Are you nervous?" I asked Xavier. I wiped a bead of sweat from his forehead with a napkin. He swatted my hand away.

"I'm not nervous," he said. "Just hot."

He tugged at the collar of his t-shirt. I burst out laughing.

"That's a terrible excuse. The AC is blasting on this plane. I'm freezing," I rubbed my arms dramatically.

Xavier sighed. "Fine. You caught me. I'm a little nervous."

"Don't worry. My parents won't hate you," I placed my hand over his and squeezed it gently. "I'll make sure they're nice to you."

He smiled and wrapped his arm around my shoulders before kissing the top of my head.

"Even if they don't like me at first," he said confidently, "I'll make sure they love me by the end of the weekend."

I rolled my eyes. My parents were going to like him. I just knew it. But they weren't the warm, openly affectionate type like his mother. Asian parents did not always show love through hugs and sweet words.

"Hi!" I waved as my brother Justin stepped out of his car. He waved back and walked toward us across the small airport parking lot.

"Hey sis," he said when he reached us. Then he turned to Xavier. "Hey man, I'm Justin."

He held out his hand.

"Xavier," Xavier replied, shaking it.

Justin grabbed my overnight bag and carried it toward his car while Xavier and I followed behind. After the guys loaded our luggage into the trunk, we climbed into the car.

"How was the flight?" Justin asked as we pulled out of the parking lot. "How many stops?"

"It was great," I said. "No stops. Nick let us use his private jet, so we flew straight here."

Justin chuckled. "Private jet? Nice."

It did not take long to reach my parents' house. When we pulled into the driveway, I paused for a moment and looked at it. This was my childhood home. My parents bought it when I was ten. They were still living there.

I moved out after graduating from grad school. Alexi moved out when she got married. Now Justin was the only one still living with them.

"I'm home!" Justin shouted as we walked inside. I heard footsteps approaching.

"Welcome home!" Mom appeared in the foyer. Then she stopped when she saw Xavier. "And who is this?"

I stepped beside Xavier and held his hand. "Mom, this is my boyfriend, Xavier."

Mom studied him for a moment before nodding politely. "Welcome to our house."

"Hello Mrs. Yang," Xavier said respectfully. Mom motioned for us to follow her into the living room. Once we sat down, she brought us cups of hot tea.

"Justin," she said, "please take Chasity's luggage to her bedroom. Her friend can sleep in the guest room."

"Yes ma'am," he replied before heading upstairs. Mom sat down across from us.

"Your father will be home soon," she said. "Then we can have dinner."

We made small talk while we waited. Mom asked the usual questions. Where was Xavier from? What he did for a living. What his parents did. How he liked New York. Justin returned after dropping off our bags in their respected rooms. Not long after that, Dad arrived home.

I introduced him to Xavier. His reaction was the same as Mom's. Calm. Polite. Neutral. I expected that. My parents would need time to warm up to him before deciding how they felt.

Later that evening, Alexi and Stephan arrived with the kids. Betty immediately ran into my arms while Josiah tried climbing onto the couch. The house quickly filled with noise, laughter, and the smell of Mom's cooking.

It felt good to be home. This was the longest I had gone without seeing my family. Thankfully, my siblings and Stephan seemed to genuinely like Xavier. After dinner, everyone slowly began getting ready for bed.

"Xavier," Justin said, clapping him on the shoulder. "Wake up early tomorrow. Like five in the morning. We're going boating and fishing. Just us guys."

Xavier nodded without hesitation. "Sounds good."

Justin disappeared into his room.

Xavier turned to me. "Good night."

He leaned down and kissed the top of my head before heading toward the guest room. I watched him go. Tomorrow morning will be the real test. Because in my family… Fishing trips were where the serious conversations happened.

Chapter 13

XAVIER

Here I was, sitting on a small fishing boat with Chasity's father, her brother Justin, and her brother-in-law Stephan. Just like Justin had warned me the night before, we had gotten up at five in the morning and driven out to the lake before the sun had even finished rising. A light mist had floated over the water when we arrived, and the cool morning air smelled faintly of pine and lake water.

Five hours later, the sun was high in the sky, the air had warmed, and the quiet hum of insects filled the shoreline. We had only caught two fish worth taking home. Personally, I had probably caught half the seaweed in the lake.

"Here you go," Justin said, handing me a small pink drink.

I turned it around in my hand curiously. The bottle was tiny, barely larger than the palm of my hand, and the bright pink plastic looked almost like a toy.

"I'm not sure what this is," I admitted.

"It's a Korean yogurt drink," Justin explained. "Sweet but not too sweet. Try it."

Well, here we went. I nodded and peeled the foil top open. A sweet, creamy scent drifted up immediately. It smelled pretty good. I tipped the bottle back and finished the drink in one gulp. Justin immediately handed me another one.

"Wow," I said, surprised. "This actually tastes really good."

Justin laughed. "Told you."

After a while, Stephan, Justin, and I started talking about football. The gentle rocking of the boat and the quiet splashing of fishing lines hitting the water created a calm rhythm around us.

We debated which teams might make it to the Super Bowl this season. Justin was convinced his team finally had a shot this year, while Stephan insisted their quarterback wasn't good enough. Meanwhile, Mr. Yang remained mostly silent. He sat at the front of the boat with quiet focus, occasionally adjusting his line and calmly reeling in fish while the rest of us struggled. Honestly, he had caught more fish than all three of us combined.

"Mom made sticky rice with Chinese sausage," Justin said suddenly. He handed me a bundle wrapped tightly in plastic wrap. I turned it over in my hands. Through the plastic I could see the ingredients, white sticky rice, slices of reddish sausage, and bits of cilantro.

"Don't worry," Justin said with a grin. "It tastes good."

I unwrapped it and took a bite. My eyes widened slightly.

"Wow," I said after swallowing. "This is really good."

I had traveled to plenty of Asian countries before and tried all kinds of food, but this sticky rice with Chinese sausage was one of the better things I had tasted. It was savory, slightly sweet, and incredibly satisfying.

"What do you do, Xavier?" Mr. Yang finally spoke. His voice was calm but firm. I swallowed the food in my mouth and cleared my throat.

"I'm a business owner," I said. "I own a chain of resorts in the United States and around the world."

"You're rich." He did not ask. It was a statement.

I nodded. "You could say that."

"Did your family pass the business on to you?" I shook my head.

"No. My father was a banker, and my mother was a stay-at-home mom. My grandparents on both sides were farmers. After I graduated from school, my best friend and I started the business together."

"Do your parents live in New York too?"

"My mom and sister do now," I said. "But my dad passed away when I was still in high school."

Mr. Yang nodded slightly. "Are you one of Joseph's friends?"

"Yes," I replied. "I've been friends with Bruce since college. When Bruce and Joe started dating, that's when I became friends with Joe."

The questions continued. Slowly. Carefully. For nearly an hour. There was no rush in his tone or sense of urgency. Somehow that made it feel more intense. Each pause between his questions felt intentional like he was giving himself time to process every answer before moving on to the next. Mr. Yang asked about my job, my family, my plans, and whether my family liked Chasity. Simple questions on the surface. But none of them felt simple sitting across from him.

Every question was calm, but every one of them carried weight. Like he was not just listening; he was evaluating. He was measuring something. Measuring me. I stayed steady, answered honestly, kept my voice even. I could feel the pressure building beneath the surface. It was not hostile. It was not unkind. But it was deliberate. And by the time the conversation stretched toward the end of that hour, I realized this was not just a casual getting to know each other conversation. It was a test.

Eventually, he seemed satisfied. The shift was subtle. It was almost easy to miss if I had not been watching so closely. Mr. Yang simply nodded once. It was a small and deliberate motion. Then he simply turned his attention back to his fishing rod as if nothing had just happened. The line cast out over the water. It was steady and undisturbed. It almost felt like the past hour had been nothing more than casual conversation. But I felt it. The release. It was the quiet signal that the interrogation was over.

I let out a breath I had not realized I'd been holding and glanced at Justin and Stephan. Stephan shrugged casually like this was all normal. I guess this was just how things normally went. Justin gave me a thumbs-up and a small grin pulled at the corner of his mouth. I let out a sigh of relief. I had made it through. I leaned back slightly as the tension in my shoulders started to ease.

"Dad approved of you," Justin whispered. The words were quiet, but they landed heavier than anything that had been said all morning. Something in my chest loosened instantly. I gave a small nod not trusting myself to say much more. Then we returned to fishing like nothing significant had just happened.

The conversation drifted easily after that. It stayed light and unstructured. Our conversations moved between nothing and everything at the same time.

They told me stories about Chasity growing up. All the small moments, inside jokes, and memories that painted a clearer picture of her I had not seen before. Stories about their cousin's adventures, about getting into trouble, and somehow, they were always getting out of it.

Stephan laughed as he told me how he had been grilled even harder than I had. How there had been higher standards for him to meet since he came from the same cultural background. There were things that he was expected to know. He shook his head, smiled, and said that I got lucky. That they would be giving me plenty of passes moving forward. I let out a quiet breath at that. The relief settled deeper this time and felt more real.

And as I continued fishing, the rhythm of it finally started to come naturally. The quiet patience. The waiting. The stillness. When I felt the slight tug on the line, I reacted quickly this time. I pulled it in with just enough confidence. A small fish broke through the surface and wriggled as I lifted it up. I let out a short laugh because I was surprised despite myself. The fish was too small to keep; it was barely anything at all, but it was still a fish regardless. And somehow, it felt like more than that.

Chapter 14

CHASITY

Since the men had gone out fishing early that morning, Alexi brought her children over to spend the day with Mom and me. The morning air was cool and fresh, carrying the earthy smell of damp soil from the garden. Sunlight filtered through the trees, warming our backs as we worked. Mom and I spent the morning pulling weeds from the vegetable beds while Alexi and the kids helped pick vegetables.

Betty carried a small basket proudly, carefully dropping tomatoes and cucumbers inside while Josiah waddled behind her trying to grab whatever he could reach. After we finished working in the garden, we washed up and had a simple lunch of leftover rice, vegetables, and soup.

Once the kids were down for their naps, the house finally became quiet again. Mom, Alexi, and I sat on the back porch, enjoying the gentle breeze before starting dinner. The porch creaked softly under our chairs, and somewhere in the distance a lawn mower hummed.

"How did you and Xavier meet?" Alexi asked curiously.

I set my drink down on the small patio table.

"We met at Joe's wedding," I replied.

"Have you met his family?" Mom asked. "What kind of people are they?"

I nodded. "I met his mom and sister a couple of months ago. His mom is sweet. His sister is married and has one daughter. His dad passed away when he was in high school."

"Are his family rich?" Mom continued, her tone curious but cautious.

I shook my head. "No. His parents were just like us. After he graduated from grad school, he started a company with his best friend. The company did well and he got rich. That's about it."

I shrugged. "His mom's house actually looks a lot like this one."

Mom nodded slowly. That seemed to ease some of her concerns. The three of us continued chatting and catching up on everything that had happened during the past few months since I moved to New York.

Before we knew it, the kids were waking up from their naps, and it was time to start preparing dinner. Soon afterward, the men returned from their fishing trip. The sun had begun its slow descent, painting the sky with soft orange and pink streaks.

"How was the fishing trip?" I asked as I sat down beside Xavier. I had been busy helping Mom cook all afternoon, so I hadn't had the chance to ask him how things went with Dad, Justin, and Stephan.

"It was good," Xavier said with a nod.

Once everyone sat down, Dad said grace before we started eating. Mom had decided to cook several traditional dishes that night. She explained that it would be a good opportunity for Xavier to try some of our family's food so he could get used to it. Thankfully, Xavier seemed to enjoy everything. Mom and Dad even began asking him more relaxed questions, and it seemed like they were finally warming up to the idea that I was dating him.

After dinner, we cleaned up the kitchen together. Then Alexi suggested we play board games and card games. The living room quickly filled with laughter as we played for hours.
Betty insisted on helping with shuffle cards even though she couldn't quite do it properly, while Josiah kept trying to steal game pieces when no one was looking.

We stayed up late playing games while my siblings and Xavier got to know each other better. Watching them all talk and laugh together made my chest feel warm. It felt good to be home. This was the longest I had been away from my family since my college years.

The end of the weekend came too quickly. Soon it was time to say goodbye. I promised my parents that I would come back for Thanksgiving and stay longer. Little Betty wrapped her arms around my leg and cried, begging me not to leave. Josiah was too young to fully understand what was happening. He simply waved his toy car around happily.

"I told you," Xavier said proudly once we were back on the private jet. The pilot had just informed us that it was safe to remove our seatbelts and move around. I smiled and shook my head.

"I told you they wouldn't hate you."

Xavier wrapped his arm around my shoulders.

"And I told you they were going to love me," he said triumphantly.

"Go ahead and take a nap. We've got a few hours before we land in New York."

"I'm good," I said, shaking my head.

"If I nap now, it'll ruin my sleep schedule. I won't be able to sleep tonight."

I opened my iPad and started scrolling through movies. It had been good seeing my family again. Catching up with Mom and Alexi was fun.

The best part was seeing my niece and nephew. Betty had always been my little shadow when I lived in Montana, so of course she missed me. Josiah, on the other hand, did not really care. I wasn't his favorite adult.

As much as I missed my family, though, I did not miss living in Montana. The cost of living was cheaper, sure. But my career had felt stagnant there. The dating pool was even worse. Most of the eligible men were guys I had gone to high school with or guys who attended the colleges in town. My parents had even tried to set me up on blind dates before. I had declined every single one.

I sighed softly as I continued to scroll through the movie options on my screen. Life in New York might be chaotic and expensive… but at least it was exciting. For the first time in a long time, my future did not feel so predictable.

*****

The host led us to the table that was always reserved for Xavier since he was the silent partner of the restaurant. On the way there, Xavier had explained how he came to be involved with the place.

The co-owner, Christof, was from a small town in Vermont. After graduating from culinary school, Christof had come to New York determined to make it big. Unfortunately, once he arrived, he quickly realized that the city was filled with incredibly talented chefs. Standing out was harder than he had imagined.

By pure chance, Christof met Xavier at one of the Warrington parties. Christof had been working there as a server. After the party, the two of them crossed paths a few more times, and Christof told Xavier about his dream of opening his own restaurant.

Nick, of course, had demanded proof. He made Christof design a full menu and cook every dish for him personally. Once Nick approved the menu, Xavier decided to invest in the restaurant. With two of the most eligible bachelors in the city frequently dining there, the restaurant quickly gained attention and soon became a popular spot for the wealthy crowd in Manhattan.

"How many of these restaurants are you secretly involved in?" I leaned forward and whispered after the host walked away.

Xavier chuckled and leaned closer. "You don't have to whisper. Not that many. I co-own about six restaurants like this."

He shrugged casually. "I'm not really interested in the food industry, so I limit myself. Otherwise, it would create too much work for Aimme. She's the one who keeps track of all the details."

I leaned back in my chair and folded my arms. "I hope you're paying Aimme well. She works way too hard."

Xavier nodded immediately. "She's one of a kind. I honestly don't know what I'd do without her."

Just then, a server arrived with water and a bottle of wine. After taking our orders, he disappeared quickly, leaving us alone again. We chatted about random things while waiting for our food.

"Well, well, well. Who do we have here?" Amber's voice rang loudly through the restaurant as she walked up behind Xavier and placed both hands on his shoulders. Xavier immediately pushed her hands away.

"What do you want?" he asked, clearly annoyed.

I tried to hide my laugh by taking a sip of water. Technically, I should have been irritated that these women kept bothering Xavier. But honestly? It was incredibly entertaining watching them embarrass themselves. They simply did not know when to stop.

At this point, I was starting to think those Korean dramas I used to watch were based on real life. Xavier rolled his eyes when he saw me covering my mouth to hide my laughter. He knew I was enjoying the show. Amber moved from behind him to stand beside our table.

"You know what I want," she said confidently. She acted as if I did not exist. Which was perfectly fine with me. I was curious to see how this would play out.

"Please leave me and my girlfriend alone," Xavier said firmly. "We would like to enjoy our dinner."

Amber placed a hand on her hip.

"What do you see in her anyway?" she demanded loudly. Her voice carried across the restaurant. "We were so in love that you asked me to marry you. Why are you with someone like her now?"

I glanced around the restaurant. Several people had already stopped eating. Others were openly staring. Amber clearly wanted an audience. And she had one. Her goal was probably to embarrass me. But something told me this might not end the way she expected.

Xavier let out a long sigh.

"I'm tired of you doing this, Amber," he said calmly. "But since you want an audience… now you have one."

He picked up his phone and tapped the screen a few times. I had no idea what he was doing. Then suddenly a voice filled the silent restaurant.

"Xavier is such a sweet guy, Amber." The sound echoed clearly from Xavier's phone. The entire restaurant fell silent. You could have heard a pin drop. Then Amber's voice played from the recording.

"He's not my type. He's a good boy. He's so boring. Always talking about all these plans, he has with Nick. Now Marshall… he's a bad boy. Everything with him is exciting. With Xavier, I'll get to be the trophy wife. I can go on vacation whenever I want with whoever I want. I'm sure he wouldn't even know. Win-win."

Laughter from her friends filled the background of the recording.

I slowly turned my head toward Amber. Her hand was covering her mouth. Her eyes burned with fury.

"I loved you, Amber," Xavier said quietly. "That's why I never told anyone the real reason I left you at the altar. The media painted me as the villain who abandoned you. I let them."

He shook his head slowly. "But you just wouldn't stop."

The restaurant erupted into whispers. I glanced around and saw people grabbing their phones. Some were typing frantically. Others were openly recording the scene. Amber spun on her heel and stormed out of the restaurant.

"Well," I said with a tight smile. "Life is certainly never dull around you."

Xavier exhaled heavily. "I'm sorry. I hope that didn't ruin our date."

"Of course not," I laughed softly and shrugged. "I'm starting to get used to this."

"When you're dating one of the most eligible bachelors in the city, you have to expect a little chaos, I guess."

Just then my phone vibrated. I pulled it out of my clutch and glanced at the screen. It wasn't text messages. It was notifications. Hundreds of them. Across various social media platforms.

"What is it?" Xavier asked. "Did something happen?"

I looked up and smiled. "You and Amber happened. I'm getting hundreds of Instagram follow requests."

I turned the screen toward him and laughed. "At this rate I might as well make my accounts public."

Xavier laughed. "I'm sorry."

At that moment the server arrived with our food. As quickly as he appeared, he disappeared again, leaving us alone to finally enjoy dinner.

Chapter 15

CHASITY

Nick had finally returned to town and wanted to hang out with Xavier. Of course, Nick wanted to hang out the *Nick way*, which usually involved clubs, loud music, and questionable life choices. Xavier immediately refused.

After some arguing, they compromised. Instead of going out, they decided to order food and hang out at my house. Which I honestly did not understand. If they wanted quality time together, shouldn't they just hang out alone? But I did not question it. Free food was free food.

"I can never have enough fried rice and orange chicken!" I announced happily as I stuffed my face. "Even though orange chicken isn't real Chinese food."

Nick and Xavier both stared at me before bursting into laughter.

"I cannot believe how easy it is to satisfy you," Nick said.

"What can I say?" I shrugged. "I'm very low maintenance."

I scooped another bite of fried rice onto my fork. "So how long are you in town for, Nick?"

"Not long," he replied with a dramatic cringe. "I'm only here for my family's monthly dinner."

He shuddered slightly. "I'm hoping Xavier will go with me."

"No," Xavier said immediately. He pointed his chopsticks at Nick. "I learned my lesson the very first time you tricked me into going with you."

Then he turned toward me. "It's a bloodbath."

"Never go with Nick to his family's monthly dinner. Whatever he offers you is not worth it."

I laughed. "I'm sure it can't be that bad."

"Oh, it is that bad," Xavier insisted, his eyes widening.

Nick straightened up in his chair.

"Fine," he said dramatically.

"If you won't go with me to dinner, then at least come with me to Florida," he leaned forward proudly. "I'm throwing a party at our resort."

Then he turned toward me and made an exaggerated pout.

"I can't," I said, shaking my head. "Classes start in a week, and I don't have the money."

"A week is all you need to have fun in Florida," Nick replied quickly. "And you're not paying for anything. I got you."

"Well…" I hesitated.

The fall semester was starting soon, and I had planned to spend the week preparing. I was teaching three courses this semester. Two in-person classes and one online course.

"If you want to go, I'll go too," Xavier said casually. Nick and I both turned to stare at him. Nick slowly broke into a huge grin.

"Oh, this is good," he said, clapping his hands together. "Come on, Chasity. You *must* go. This is the first time my boy here is willingly going on a vacation."

He clasped his hands together dramatically. "Please go to Florida with me!"

I leaned back and thought about it. I had been to Florida several times before, so I wouldn't need to do much sightseeing. Most of the time would probably be spent on the beach.
And honestly… I could use some sun.

"Okay," I finally said. "I'll go."

"Yes!" Nick shouted, punching the air. "We leave tonight after my family dinner."

He pointed at us. "Meet me at the airport at nine."

I shook my head, laughing. I had no idea what kind of family Nick had, but I couldn't believe he wanted to leave tonight. He had just flown into New York that morning. When we met his parents before, they seemed perfectly friendly and welcoming. After we finished eating, we cleaned up the kitchen. Nick hung out for another few hours before heading to his parents' house for dinner.

Once he left, I started packing. We were only going to be gone for a week, so I did not need much. I tossed a few sundresses, shorts, t-shirts, and my swimsuit into my suitcase.

Meanwhile, Xavier did the smart thing. He called his housekeeper. By the time his driver arrived to pick us up, his luggage was already perfectly packed and waiting. Lucky man. I zipped my suitcase closed and dragged it to the front door.

"Ready?" Xavier asked.

I nodded. "Ready."

Florida, here we come.

*****

I couldn't believe I was in Florida. For the past few days since we landed, I had done almost nothing except lie on the beach. My skin had been beautifully kissed by the sun, leaving behind a warm golden glow. It had been so long since I had allowed myself to truly relax.
I stretched out on the private cabana, letting the gentle ocean breeze brush across my skin. The salty scent of the sea mixed with the faint sweetness of sunscreen and coconut oil drifting through the air.

I had no idea where Nick and Xavier had disappeared to, but that wasn't my problem. Right now, I am perfectly content. I watched as people walked along the shoreline, some laughing as waves crashed against their legs while others lounged in chairs under colorful umbrellas. A group of kids splashed loudly in the water while couples strolled hand in hand along the beach. Nothing made me happier than people watching, enjoying the warm weather, and reading.

I reached into my beach bag and pulled out my Kindle. Lately I have been completely lost in romance novels. They transported me into worlds where problems could be solved within a few hundred pages and where love always found a way. It was comforting. Safe. Especially after everything that happened recently.

Ever since the restaurant showdown between Xavier and Amber, gossip articles exploded across the internet. Amber had practically vanished off the face of the earth, while Xavier seemed to be followed everywhere by paparazzi. They occasionally tried to take pictures of me too or shout questions as I walked past. But I ignored them. Eventually they lost interest. After all, I lived a pretty boring middle-class life compared to the glamorous circles Xavier moved in.

"Miss, I have a drink here for you," the sudden voice startled me. I hadn't even seen the server approaching. I sat up and took the drink from him. The glass was cold against my fingers, condensation already sliding down the sides.

"Thanks," I said slowly, setting the drink on the small table beside me. "But I didn't order this."

"Someone else ordered and paid for it, ma'am," the server replied politely. He handed me a small card. "The gentleman asked me to give this to you."

Oh. Maybe it was from Xavier or Nick. That was kind of sweet. I opened the card. At first, I only skimmed it. Then my stomach dropped. I must have read it wrong. My fingers trembled slightly as I picked the card back up and forced myself to read the words again, slowly this time.

You can run, but you can't hide, babe.
Enjoy the sun and this drink.
Soon we'll be together again.

The blood drained from my face. He found me. He was here. I shot up from the cabana and looked around frantically. The beach was crowded. Too many people. Too many umbrellas. Too many faces. I wouldn't be able to spot him even if he was standing right in front of me.

But he could see me. He could be anywhere. He could be sitting behind one of the umbrellas. Standing near the bar. Or worse… Watching me from one of the hundreds of hotel rooms towering above the beach. Looking down at me. Waiting.

I knew he would find me eventually. But I had hoped, just for a few days, I could pretend he did not exist. Just long enough to breathe again. My chest tightened. My pulse began racing. I couldn't stay here. I needed to get back to the room. Now.

I shoved my Kindle into my bag and hurriedly stuffed everything else inside. My hands were shaking so badly I nearly dropped my phone. I slung the bag over my shoulder and turned to leave.

"Woah! Where's the fire?" Xavier's voice suddenly stopped me as I ran straight into him. I stumbled back slightly.

"Oh… sorry," I muttered quickly. "I'm just heading back to the room."

"Already?" Nick said, stepping up behind him. "We just got here."

I opened my mouth to answer. But nothing came out. My chest tightened even more. My breathing became shallow. Too fast. Too uneven. Oh no. Not now. My heart was pounding violently against my ribs.

I tried to slow my breathing. Deep breaths. I knew the techniques. I taught them. Deep breath in. Hold. Exhale. Find your safe place. Calm your body. But it wasn't working.

My heart wouldn't slow down. The sound of the ocean faded. The voices around me blurred into distant noise. My vision started narrowing. Dark spots crept into the edges of my sight.

No. This was bad. This was really bad. I tried to grab Xavier's arm. But before I could say anything… Everything went black.

* * * * *

"How is she doing, doctor?" I heard Xavier's voice somewhere nearby. Where were we? Who was he talking to? My eyelids felt heavy as I slowly opened them. The bright sunlight that had been shining over the beach was gone. Instead, soft yellow lighting filled the room. I blinked a few times, trying to focus.

I was lying in a large bed. The familiar cream-colored walls and ocean-view balcony slowly came into focus. Our hotel room. Wasn't I just at the cabana? My head spun. I tried to sit up but immediately felt dizzy.

"Woah, easy there," Nick said quickly, reaching forward to help me. He gently guided me into a sitting position. He was sitting at the edge of the bed, watching me carefully. I rubbed my temples as a dull ache pulsed behind my eyes.

"Weren't we just at the cabana?" I asked slowly. "Why am I here?"

"Xavier's talking to the doctor outside," Nick explained calmly. "But yeah… you fainted at the cabana."

He handed me a glass of water. "We brought you back here."

I took a sip. The cool water helped clear the dryness in my throat. Just then the door opened. Xavier rushed into the room. The moment he saw me sitting up, his eyes widened.

"Why are you up already?" he exclaimed. "You should still be lying down!"

He hurried to my side just as Nick stood up.

"I'm going to leave you two," Nick said quietly. He nodded toward Xavier before slipping out of the room and closing the door behind him.

Xavier immediately pulled me into a tight hug.

"I'm okay," I muttered, pushing lightly against his chest. "Stop acting like that. I'm fine."

He finally released me but stayed close.

"The doctor said you fainted from exhaustion," he said gently, brushing a strand of hair behind my ear. "You scared me."

His voice softened. "My heart nearly stopped when you collapsed."

"I'm okay now," I said, swatting his hand away lightly.

Xavier sat back, though his eyes were still studying me carefully.

"Do you need anything?" he asked. "I can call room service and have lunch brought up."

"Sure," I replied quietly."Anything is fine. I think I'm going to take a nap."

I slowly lay back down on the bed and turned onto my side.

"I'll let you know when the food arrives," Xavier said softly. He patted my hair before standing. Then he walked out of the room, closing the door behind him. The moment the door clicked shut, I rolled onto my back and pressed my fingers against my temples.

My heart began to race again. I couldn't believe it. He was here. Here. In Florida. Watching me. Of course he found me. Money talked. And money made things happen. If someone had enough of it, they could reach anywhere.

I had hoped that maybe… just maybe… I could lose him for a while. Even for a few days. Just enough time to breathe. Just enough time to pretend he did not exist. But I had been too optimistic. Too hopeful.

My stomach twisted into a knot. What am I supposed to do now? I stared at the ceiling, my mind racing. I needed a plan. And I needed one quickly. Because if I did not… History might repeat itself. And this time, I wasn't sure I would survive it again.

Chapter 16

XAVIER

I hadn't realized how exhausted Chasity had been. So much had changed in her life within the past few months. She moved across the country, started a new job, and was adjusting to a completely different lifestyle. On top of that, she had been stressed about money ever since she moved to New York. The cost of living there was nothing like Montana.

I should have gone to the cabana with her this morning. But Nick insisted on dragging me to the gym to work out and spar.

"Argh!" I groaned as I grabbed one of the accent pillows from the couch and hurled it at the wall. I ran a hand through my hair. What could I do to help her relax? Then it hit me. The spa. Of course. It wouldn't magically remove all her stress, but it would help.

I grabbed my phone and called the spa located on the third floor of the resort. After a short conversation, I booked Chasity the most expensive spa package they offered. Full body massage, facial, aromatherapy, everything. She deserved it. Just as I ended the call, the doorbell rang.

Room service. I walked over and opened the door. A server stood there with a cart full of covered dishes.

"Where would you like this, sir?" he asked politely as he rolled the cart inside.

"Right here is fine," I said, pointing toward the sitting area. I handed him a tip.

"Thank you, sir," he said with a quick nod before leaving the suite. I pushed the cart toward the bedroom and knocked gently on the door before opening it.

"Room service just delivered your food," I announced.

Chasity slowly sat up in bed. Her hair was slightly messy from sleep, and she still looked pale.

"Thanks for getting food for me," she said softly as she climbed out of bed and walked over to the cart. "I appreciate it."

"I'll let you eat," I said. "Oh, and I scheduled a spa appointment for you at three."

She immediately shook her head. "Oh, you didn't have to."

"I know," I replied gently. "But today proved how stressed you've been. The spa won't solve everything, but it'll help you relax a little."

I smiled. "And you can write a review about it."

She sighed but eventually smiled. "Fine, whatever."

She waved her hand at me dismissively. I leaned down and kissed the top of her head before stepping back. "Enjoy your lunch."

Chapter 17

CHASITY

I waited until Xavier closed the door behind him before lifting the silver cover from the tray. The smell of warm food immediately filled the room. Steam curled gently into the air from the plate. The food was still hot, so I picked up the spoon and began eating quickly. My stomach reminded me just how hungry I was. I had only taken a few bites when something caught my eye.

A small, folded piece of white paper sat beside the plate. My hand froze. Slowly, I reached for it. My fingers trembled slightly as I unfolded the paper. The words were written in neat, familiar handwriting.

Eat up, my love.
You need your energy.
We will be together very soon.

The room suddenly felt colder. My appetite vanished instantly. The spoon slipped from my hand and clattered softly against the plate.

He was here.

Not just somewhere in the resort. Close. Close enough to reach my room. Close enough to send messages. My chest tightened as a wave of fear rushed through me. He was bold. Bolder than before.

But I refused to let him win. Not again. Not this time. I wasn't the same frightened girl I had been years ago. I am older now. Stronger. Smarter. But then again… So was he.

I let out a slow breath and leaned back into the chair, staring at the note in my hand. Fear wouldn't help me. Panic wouldn't help me. What I needed was a plan. And I needed to think clearly.

I glanced back at the plate of food. If I was going to come up with a plan… I needed energy. I picked the spoon back up and forced myself to take another bite. Maybe the spa appointment Xavier booked wasn't such a bad idea after all. If I could calm my mind for a little while, maybe I could figure out what to do next.

Because one thing was certain. He wasn't going to ruin me again. And he wasn't going to ruin my life.

Chapter 18

XAVIER

Chasity was at her spa appointment, and I was sitting with Nick in one of the private cabanas overlooking the beach. The ocean stretched endlessly in front of us, waves rolling onto the shore in a steady rhythm. The salty breeze drifted through the cabana, carrying the sound of laughter and music from other guests relaxing nearby.

For that moment, everything seemed calm. We were just killing time before the party tonight. Personally, I did not want to go. But Chasity wanted to attend with Nick, so I did not have much of a choice.

"Man," Nick said, leaning back in his lounge chair, "you are whipped."

He chuckled and shook his head. "You two haven't even been dating that long."

I slowly turned my head and glared at him from behind my sunglasses.

"You're crazy," I replied. "I am not *whipped*."

I even made air quotes with my fingers.

Nick burst out laughing. "Sure. Sure. Whatever you say, man."

He lifted his drink and took a sip. "But I think she's the one for you."

I did not respond right away. Nick continued talking. "You've been happier these last few months than I've seen you in years."

He pointed a finger at me. "You stopped working late. You stopped working weekends. And now you're on vacation."

He laughed again. "I mean… who are you and what did you do with the real Xavier?"

I leaned back in my chair and stared out at the ocean. Nick wasn't wrong. Everything had changed. And it all started the moment I saw her. I still remember that day clearly.

Bruce and Joe's wedding. The music. The flowers. The crowd stood as the wedding party began walking down the aisle. Then I saw her.

Chasity.

Walking slowly down the aisle in her bridesmaid dress. The moment my eyes landed on her, something inside me shifted. I couldn't explain it. I did not need to. I just knew. I was completely and utterly done for.

* * * * *

Nick and I entered the ballroom, and we both stopped in our tracks. I finally understood why Joe had nearly gone insane trying to plan this wedding. The decorations were breathtaking.
From the ceiling all the way down to the floor, everything was designed with incredible attention to detail. Crystal chandeliers shimmered under the warm lights, and elegant floral arrangements lined the walls and tables. The soft color scheme blended perfectly, creating an atmosphere that felt both luxurious and intimate.

It was phenomenal.

Nick nudged my side and tilted his head toward the open bar. We grabbed glasses of whiskey before making our way upstairs to Bruce's suite.

"There you guys are," Bruce said with a laugh when he opened the door. Nick and I stepped inside, closing the door behind us. Nick immediately made his way toward the couches in the center of the room.

On the coffee table sat several boutonnieres waiting to be pinned onto our tuxedos. We took turns helping each other attach them before settling down on the couches. For the next half hour, the three of us talked about absolutely nothing important while snacking on the impressive spread of food laid out on a side table. Eventually, the wedding planner knocked on the door and told us it was time.

Soft music was already playing when we entered the ceremony space. The officiant walked gracefully to the small altar that had been built specifically for the wedding. Nick and I walked ahead of Bruce, slowly making our way down the aisle. Once we reached the front, Bruce took his place beside the officiant while Nick and I moved to stand slightly behind him.

I couldn't stop smiling. I was genuinely happy for Bruce and Joe. Their relationship had taken years to get here. They had survived countless ups and downs together. If anyone deserved this kind of happiness… It was them.

The music shifted. I glanced up as Joe's wedding party began walking down the aisle. Black heels stepped gracefully onto the white aisle runner. Then a long sweep of black fabric followed behind them. My eyes slowly traveled upward. And then…

Time stopped.

My heart nearly skipped a beat. She was the most beautiful woman I had ever seen.

Her face was softly oval-shaped, framed by delicate features. Her large brown eyes seemed to sparkle under the lights, and a small, perfectly shaped nose sat above full red lips. Her hair was pulled back into a sleek high bun, revealing the elegant curve of her neck. She smiled brightly as she glided slowly down the aisle.

The moment felt surreal. Like the entire room had faded away. Instinctively, my eyes dropped down to her hands. I searched desperately for a ring on her left ring finger. But I couldn't see clearly. Her right hand rested lightly over the other, partially hiding it.

"You need to breathe," Nick whispered quietly in my ear. "I can't have you fainting on me before the party even begins."

I blinked. Only then did I realize I had been holding my breath. I slowly exhaled.

* * * * *

"Shots! Shots! Shots!" Nick shouted over the music as we stood in our suite getting ready. He lined up three glasses on the counter and poured liquor into them.

"We've already had three!" Chasity protested, laughing.

"This is my last one or I'm not making it to the party. I'm a foot shorter than both of you!" She was already getting tipsy. Her cheeks were flushed and she was much more animated than usual.

We threw back the shots anyway. The alcohol burned all the way down my throat. God, I was getting too old for this.

Music pounded through the speakers. Lights flashed across the pool. The entire place was buzzed with energy. Nick loved this kind of chaos. I tolerated it.

People were dancing. Others lounged around the pool with drinks in hand. Some were already swimming.

Nick was immediately pulled away by a group of women the moment we stepped outside. Typical. I reached for Chasity's hand so she wouldn't disappear into the crowd. But when I looked down… She wasn't there.

I scanned the area. Then I spotted her at the bar. She must have gotten separated from us in the crowd. I started heading toward her. Then someone grabbed my arm.

"Xavier!" I groaned internally.

Maggie.

"I didn't know you were going to be here!" she shouted over the music.

"Sure, you didn't," I muttered as I tried pulling my arm away. "Let go. I need to go."

But she wrapped her arms around my torso. "I missed you!"

Then she tried to kiss me. She was drunk. I grabbed her shoulders and pushed her away.

"Stop embarrassing yourself, Maggie," I snapped. "I don't like you. Stop throwing yourself at me."

Then I walked away without another word. I heard her shriek behind me, but I did not bother looking back. I was done with her.

"Hey," I said when I reached Chasity. "What happened to you?"

"I'm short, remember?" she replied. "You and Nick ditched me."

"Sorry," I said, wrapping my arm around her shoulders and kissing her temple. We grabbed drinks and moved around the party. I introduced her to a few people I knew, and eventually Nick reappeared and dragged her away to meet more guests.

"I'll be back!" Chasity told me. "I'm going to the bathroom."

I nodded.

* * * * *

Thirty minutes passed. Chasity hadn't returned. I frowned. She wasn't that drunk. Even if there was a line, she shouldn't have gone this long. Something felt wrong.

I walked inside the hotel to look for her. I asked one of the female staff members to check the restroom. She came back a few minutes later.

"She's not in there."

My stomach dropped. Where could she be? Did she go back to our suite? Maybe she got tired. I rushed to the elevator and went upstairs. But she wasn't in the suite either. Now I was starting to panic. Where the hell was she?

"Mister Sterling!" The hotel manager ran toward me the moment I stepped off the elevator. "Come quickly!"

She led me down a hallway toward a side door. Then I saw her.

Chasity.

She was lying motionless at the bottom of the staircase. One of the housekeepers stood beside her.

"Who did this to her?!" I shouted as I ran down the stairs.

I reached for her—

But the manager grabbed my arm. "Don't move her!"

Right. Her neck. If she had a spinal injury, moving her could paralyze her. The housekeeper collapsed onto the ground crying.

"I'm sorry. I came out for my break and found her. I ran to get the manager."

"Call an ambulance!" I ordered.

"They're already on the way," the manager replied.

My mind raced. Did she trip over something? Or did someone push her? None of this made sense.

"Get the camera footage!" I shouted. "I need to know what happened!"

"Yes sir. Security is already pulling it," she said before running toward the lobby to meet the paramedics.

I knelt beside Chasity and carefully took her hand.

"Baby…" I whispered. I'm so sorry this happened. You're going to be okay."

The paramedics arrived quickly. They stabilized her neck and loaded her onto the stretcher. I climbed into the ambulance with them. There was no way I was letting her go alone.

At the hospital, she was examined in the emergency room before being moved to the private wing. Nick and I had funded the wing when we built the resort.

"How is she?" I asked the doctor when he returned.

"Well," the doctor said, checking his chart. "She has a concussion and a broken wrist. We'll know more once she wakes up. I gave her medication, so she'll sleep through the night."

"I understand," I said.

Then the door burst open. Nick rushed in, out of breath. "What happened?"

"She fell down the stairs," I said quietly. "Concussion and broken wrist."

Nick ran a hand over his face. "Shit. We need to call Joe."

I nodded. Her parents did not need to know yet. Not until we understood how serious this was.

"They'll kill me if they find out I let this happen to her," I muttered.

"You mean they'll kill me," Nick said dryly. "I'm the one who convinced her to come."

He called Joe and explained everything.

"They're flying here now," Nick said after hanging up.

* * * * *

My phone buzzed. The security footage. Nick moved beside me as I pressed play.

The video showed Chasity leaving the restroom. She turned right. Then suddenly he spun around and ran toward the side door. A moment later… Maggie came out of the restroom and followed her.

"Shit," I muttered. "It was Maggie."

Nick shook his head. "We can't accuse her without proof. You know who her father is. He'd crush us."

"I know."

Nick grabbed the phone again. "Wait."

He replayed the video.

"There's something off about this."

"What?" I asked..

"For a split second," Nick said slowly, "she saw something. Or someone. She wasn't running from Maggie. She was running from something else."

Nick immediately pulled out his phone. "Ian, get me every camera angle from that hallway."

Then he looked at me. "You know Chasity's house?"

"Of course," I said. "I renovated it."

Nick nodded slowly. "I created the trust for it."

My stomach dropped. "What?"

Nick began pacing. "Joe asked me to do it. I thought it was weird. Why would Joe need me to create a trust for his cousin?"

"That's why you came back for the charity event," I said.

Nick nodded. "I knew you were still hung up on her. But something about this situation didn't feel right."

He stopped pacing. "Why does a professor need her house protected by a legal trust?"

*****

Hours later, Joe and Bruce arrived.

"How is she?" Joe asked immediately.

"She's stable," I said. "Concussion and broken wrist."

Joe sat beside her and held her hand.

"You should get some rest," he told me. Bruce guided me to the family room. I collapsed onto the couch. I hadn't realized how exhausted I was. Within minutes, I was asleep. But one question kept echoing in my mind. What was really going on with Chasity?

Chapter 19

CHASITY

"You bitch!" I looked up into the mirror and saw Maggie walking up behind me.

I smiled faintly. "I thought you didn't converse with people who were below you?"

She pointed a finger at me. "You are the reason why Xavier has been ignoring me lately!"

I shrugged as I finished washing my hands and accepted a towel from the restroom attendant. "Thank you."

I tossed the towel into the basket by the door and walked out. The moment the restroom door closed behind me, the hair on my arms stood up. He was here. He was close.

Everything suddenly felt like it was moving in slow motion. I turned my head to the right. And there he was. Still handsome. Still perfect. Just like he had always been. He wore a simple T-shirt and shorts, blending into the crowd like any other guest. But his eyes were locked onto me. Then he smiled. And waved.

My heart slammed against my ribs. I had to run. I couldn't be caught. Not again.

I spun around and spotted an exit to my left. My body reacted before my brain could think. I burst through the door. Cool air hit my skin and for a brief second, I felt like I could breathe again.

"You think you can run away from me?" I turned around. Maggie stood behind me. Relief rushed through me. It was only Maggie. I exhaled slowly and shook my head.

"Really? You had to follow me?"

"You think you can have Xavier?" she snapped. "Well, you thought wrong. He's mine. He's been mine for years."

She planted her hands on her hips.

I laughed.

She was so stupid. Why chase someone who clearly had no interest in her? Well, I knew why. Xavier had money. Marrying him meant a lifetime as a trophy wife. It had been easy for her to stalk him while he was single all those years.

"I wasn't even interested in Xavier," I said casually. "But you know what? He followed me around like a little lost puppy despite how many times I turned him down."

I tilted my head. "And he's yours? If he really was, he wouldn't be living with me. Yours my ass."

"You bitch!" Maggie raised her hand like she was about to slap me, but she hesitated.

I laughed again. "Oh, you didn't know? We've been living together for a few months now."

Her face turned bright red. I placed a hand over my chest dramatically. "Oh, my goodness. I'm so sorry you're only finding out now."

Then Maggie shoved me. Hard. I lost my footing. The stairs vanished beneath me. And I started tumbling. Everything went black.

*****

Beep. Beep. Beep.

What was that annoying sound? Probably my alarm. I tried to open my eyes, but my eyelids felt like they weighed a thousand pounds. I tried moving my hands.

"Chasity?"

That sounded like Joe. Why was Joe in Florida? Were he and Bruce on vacation too? I tried again and finally managed to open my eyes.

"Joe?" My throat burned. "Water."

"Here." He placed a straw against my lips. The water was cool and refreshing. It felt amazing sliding down my throat. Only then did I realize how dry and cracked my lips felt.

"Do you have Chapstick?" I croaked. "My lips feel so dry."

Joe dug through his backpack and gently applied Chapstick to my lips.

"Thank you."

"How are you feeling?" he asked softly, brushing my hair away from my forehead. I looked around. White walls. Machines. Hospital equipment. I wasn't in the suite. I was in a hospital room.

"Confused," I admitted. "And in pain. How did I get here?"

Joe squeezed my hand.

"You fell down a staircase at the hotel," he said. "You have a concussion and a broken wrist."

"Oh." That explained the pounding headache.

"Also," Joe muttered darkly, "you were drunk. So, whoever did this to you is going to pay."

I laughed weakly, wincing as it hurt my throat. "Oh Joe, how I've missed you. I may be physically hurt, but someone else was emotionally and mentally destroyed. My wounds will heal. Hers might not."

"Who?" he asked.

"Maggie."

Joe shot to his feet. "She pushed you?"

"We exchanged a few words," I said, making air quotes with my fingers. "She was angry. She pushed me."

I shrugged carefully. "I'm fine. But the look on her face? Totally worth it."

Joe waved his arms in frustration. "How is this fine?!"

I tried to sit up but couldn't, so I grabbed the remote and raised the hospital bed.

"Okay fine. It's not fine," I sighed. "We argued. She pushed me down the stairs. I got a concussion and a broken wrist. What can I do? She's a rich spoiled girl. I'm just some poor kid from Montana."

Joe crossed his arms. "Well now you have powerful people behind you. Bruce will handle this."

"Did I hear my name?" Bruce poked his head into the room. "Oh! Welcome back to the land of the living, Chasity."

"Why thank you," I smiled.

"Honey," Joe said seriously, "Maggie pushed Chasity down those stairs. We cannot have that disgusting leech hurting our family."

Bruce nodded slowly. "I'll have a word with her father. Before the police get here."

Then he left the room.

"Let me order you some breakfast," Joe picked up the phone. He ordered what sounded like enough food to feed twenty people. "I'll go tell lover boy you're awake."

Then he disappeared.

I took a slow breath. Maggie was the least of my worries. He was back. In my life. Not by my choice. He was at the hotel yesterday. Watching me. He was following me. Smiling.

This meant he knew. He knew I lived in New York. He probably knew where I worked. He probably even knew I was dating Xavier. I never wanted to bring this crazy bastard into Xavier's life. But I already had.

* * * * *

A knock sounded at the door. Finally. Food.

"Come in!" I called. Xavier walked in first. Nick followed behind him. They both looked freshly showered and changed.

"How are you feeling?" Xavier asked as he sat beside me on the bed. Nick took Joe's old chair.

"Hungry," I said. "Even in the private wing the food still takes forever."

Nick shrugged. "Better menu though."

Xavier took my hand and kissed the back of it. His eyes looked sad. Worried.

"How was the rest of the party?" I asked.

"No idea," Nick said.

"We've been here all night. No police were called so I guess it ended fine."

"You stayed here all night?" I asked.

Xavier nodded. "I rode in the ambulance with you. Nick cleaned up the mess and came after. He called Joe and Bruce. They got here around four this morning."

"How did you find me?" I asked.

"I didn't," Xavier admitted. He rubbed the back of his neck. "One of the housekeepers did. I'm sorry, Chasity. This is my fault. I should have told Maggie off a long time ago."

"How did you know it was Maggie?" I asked.

"Security footage," Nick answered. "She followed you out the side door."

"Oh."

"We'll take care of it," Nick added.

I shook my head. "No need. Bruce already handled it."

"My man!" Nick clapped his hands.

Right then the nutritionist brought in my food.

"Finally!" I exclaimed. "I'm starving!"

I started eating immediately. Thankfully my left wrist was broken. If it had been my dominant hand, I'd be doomed.

"Slow down," Nick laughed. "No one is stealing your food."

Xavier stayed quiet. Watching me. Thinking.

* * * * *

Later Joe returned.

"Do you want me to call your mom or sister?" he asked.

"No," I said quickly. "My mom would have a heart attack."

"But—"

"No buts," I interrupted. "You remember what happened last time."

Joe's expression darkened. Nick perked up. "What happened last time?"

"Nothing," I said lightly. "My mom had a scare and ended up in the hospital."

Joe stood. "Can we have a minute?"

The others nodded and stepped out. Joe switched to our native language.

"You need to tell her," he said quietly. "This isn't like last time. Last time she was in the hospital because you were kidnapped. You were kidnapped for six damn months."

"Joe," I whispered. "He's here."

Joe froze. "What? That should've been the first thing you said this morning!"

He started pacing. "What do we do?"

"I don't know," I whispered. "I saw him yesterday. He smiled at me. He knew exactly where we were staying."

Tears spilled down my face. Joe pulled me into a hug. "I'm telling Xavier. And you're moving into his condo. It's not safe for you to stay at your house."

I nodded. He was probably right. The guys strolled back in.

"What's wrong?" Xavier rushed to me, cupping my face.

Joe took a deep breath. “There’s something we’ve been hiding.”

“You guys aren’t actually cousins?” Nick joked.

Bruce elbowed him. Joe turned to Nick. “Remember when I asked you to create that trust for Chasity’s house?”

Nick nodded. “Yes.”

Joe exhaled slowly. “Chasity has a stalker. She’s been running from him for years. And he’s here in Florida. That’s what she saw last night. That’s why she ran. And Maggie just happened to push her.”

The room went silent.

“You have a stalker?” Xavier asked quietly.

“I knew it!” Nick said. “That explains the trust, the house, the missing social media, everything.”

Xavier looked back at me. “Who is he? How long has he been stalking you?”

Joe shook his head. “This isn’t my story.”

Xavier’s voice softened. “Tell us what you’re comfortable telling.”

I took a deep breath. Maybe Joe was right. Maybe it was time to stop running.

“His name is Ryan,” I said. “I met him my freshman year of college. At first, he seemed perfect. Charming. Kind. Sweet. But I did not like him the way he liked me. He followed me everywhere. After two semesters, Joe told me to shut it down. So, I did. And that’s when everything changed.”

Then the flood gates opened.

Chapter 20

CHASITY

Jared waved goodbye to me as we headed toward our cars. The wide brick steps of the university library were behind us, glowing softly under the tall iron lampposts that lined the main walkway. Students were still scattered across the campus even though the library had just closed for the night. Some were sitting on the grass beneath the large oak trees that shaded the quad during the day, while others hurried across the paved paths with backpacks slung over their shoulders, trying to beat the cool night air settling over the campus.

Luckily, Jared had found parking right in front of the library along the curb that ran beside the long stone building. The tall glass windows of the library reflected the golden campus lights, and the quiet hum of late-night studying still lingered in the air. Me? Not so lucky. I had to park in the student lot up the street, past the row of academic buildings and the small courtyard fountain that bubbled quietly in the center of campus.

Still, I was glad I had picked up this shift. It meant extra money to add to my savings. I needed to save as much as possible to pay off my student loans. I sighed as I adjusted the strap of my bag and started walking toward the parking lot.

Joe better have made dinner tonight instead of ogling his study partner again.

"Hi, beautiful."

My entire body froze. I knew that voice. Ryan. Why couldn't he just give up? Did he have no dignity?

"Ryan," I said without even looking at him, continuing to walk. "I told you already. I don't like you. Stop following me around. You're only going to hurt yourself."

Then everything went black.

* * * * *

My head pounded. For a moment I thought maybe I was getting sick. Slowly, I opened my eyes.

The ceiling above me wasn't the cracked white plaster of my tiny apartment. Instead, dark wooden beams stretched across a high vaulted ceiling. A large chandelier hung in the center of the room; its warm light dimmed to a soft glow. Panic surged through me.

I pushed myself up slightly and looked around.

The bedroom was huge, far bigger than any room in my apartment. The bed beneath me was massive, a king-sized bed with thick white bed sheets and a heavy dark-green comforter. The headboard was carved wood, polished and expensive looking, and the bedposts were tall, thick columns that rose almost to the ceiling. A plush cream-colored rug spread across the hardwood floor, soft enough that my bare feet would have sunk into it.

Across the room stood a large dresser with a wide mirror above it. A leather armchair sat beside a tall window draped in heavy curtains that blocked out most of the daylight. Next to it was a bookshelf filled with neatly arranged novels and magazines. Everything in the room looked clean, organized, and strangely luxurious.

But the beauty of the room only made my stomach twist harder.

Because I did not belong here.

I looked down at my hands.

Chains.

Cold metal wrapped tightly around my wrists and was secured to the thick wooden bedpost. My legs were chained too, the heavy links locked around my ankles and fastened to the opposite post. The metal clinked softly when I moved, reminding me that no matter how big or beautiful the room was, it was still a cage.

Fuck.

Ryan.

Joe had warned me that he was crazy. I had thought Ryan was just a harmless guy who couldn't get over his crush.

"Good morning, beautiful." Ryan walked into the bedroom smiling.

I glared at him. "What are you doing, Ryan?"

"Bringing you breakfast in bed," he said casually, placing a tray on the nightstand. He sat beside me and began cutting up pancakes and eggs. "I didn't want you to be hungry."

I said nothing. He held up a piece of pancake to my mouth. I kept my lips shut.

"What's wrong?" he asked.

"Maybe because I'm lying down?" I replied flatly. "I can't swallow food in this position."

Ryan stood up and unlocked the chains around my legs. Then he unlocked one of my hands, leaving the other still chained.

"Better?" he asked.

I nodded slowly and pushed myself into a sitting position. The chains around my wrist clinked softly against the bedpost as I moved. Ryan adjusted the tray and began cutting the pancakes into small pieces before lifting the fork toward my mouth. I forced myself to open my mouth and chew.

The pancakes were warm and sweet, the eggs buttery and soft. Under normal circumstances it would have been a nice breakfast. But every bite felt heavy in my mouth, like I was swallowing rocks. My stomach churned with fear and anger, yet I forced myself to keep eating.

If the food wasn't poisoned, I needed it. I needed energy. Energy meant my mind could stay sharp. Energy meant I could think clearly instead of letting panic take over. And I needed to think. I needed a plan.

Throwing a tantrum or screaming at him would only make things worse. Ryan clearly believed he was doing something romantic or normal. If I fought him now, he would only tighten the chains or hurt me. Worse, he might move me somewhere even harder to escape from.

So, I swallowed my pride along with the food. I kept my breathing steady and my face calm, pretending that none of this terrified me. Inside, my thoughts were racing, examining every detail of the room, every movement Ryan made, every sound outside the walls.

I couldn't afford to be emotional. I had to stay logical. I had to stay sharp. Because the moment an opportunity appeared, I needed to be ready to take it.

*****

After I finished eating, Ryan gathered the empty plates and utensils from the tray. The metal chains clinked softly as I shifted on the bed, watching him carefully. He balanced the tray on one hand and walked out of the bedroom, closing the door behind him with a quiet click.

The room fell silent. Too silent.

I listened closely, trying to pick up any sounds beyond the door, footsteps, voices, anything that might tell me where I was or if anyone else was in the house. But there was nothing. Just the faint hum of what sounded like a ventilation system somewhere in the walls.

Minutes passed. I had no idea how long he had gone. Time felt strange here, stretching and folding in on itself. Then the door opened again. Ryan stepped back into the room, smiling as if nothing about this situation was unusual.

"Would you like a tour of the house?" he asked casually, leaning against the doorframe for a moment before walking toward the bed.

I nodded. I had to be careful. Every movement, every word, every reaction mattered now. Ryan walked behind me and leaned down close to my ear. I felt his breath brush against my skin.

"I just want to warn you," he whispered softly before pressing a kiss to my forehead, "if you try to run away, things will get worse."

His voice wasn't angry. It was calm. That somehow made it more terrifying.

"I just want us to be together."

"Okay," I said quietly, forcing my voice to remain steady. He smiled again, clearly pleased with my response.

Ryan bent down and unlocked the chains around my ankles first. The heavy metal links slid off my skin with a dull clank as they fell against the bedpost. Then he unlocked one of the cuffs around my wrists and removed it completely before unlocking the other.

The sudden freedom felt strange.

I slowly swung my legs off the bed and rubbed my wrists and ankles where the metal had dug into my skin. Red marks circled them like bruised bracelets. Standing up made my head spin for a second. I hadn't realized how stiff my body had become from lying there. Ryan watched me carefully, his eyes following every movement as if he were studying me.

"After the tour…" I said cautiously, brushing my fingers through my greasy hair, "can I take a shower?"

I could feel the oil building on my scalp and the stickiness of sweat on my skin. My clothes smelled like the library from the night before. "My hair feels disgusting."

Ryan's expression softened immediately.

"Of course, love," he said warmly, as if granting me a simple favor instead of holding me prisoner. He reached out and lightly brushed a strand of hair away from my face before gesturing toward the bedroom door. "Come on. Let me show you your new home."

*****

Later, I stood in front of the large bathroom vanity staring at the neatly arranged bottles and jars spread across the marble countertop. The bathroom itself was enormous, almost the size of my entire bedroom back in my apartment. Soft yellow lights framed the wide mirror, and the polished stone floor felt cold beneath my bare feet. A glass shower stood in one corner and a deep soaking tub sat beneath a small, frosted window.

But none of that mattered. My attention was locked on the products in front of me.

Ryan was a sociopath. There was no other explanation.

Every single skincare product sitting on the vanity was exactly what I used. The same brand of cleanser. The same toner. The same moisturizer. Even the same sunscreen I kept in the small basket on my bathroom counter back home.

My stomach twisted. There was no way he could know that unless he had broken into my apartment. He must have been watching me for months… maybe even longer than that. My fingers trembled slightly as I applied the moisturizer to my face, forcing myself to breathe slowly. Panic would only make things worse.

Then I heard it.

The bedroom door opened. And closed.

Ryan.

My heart skipped, but I forced my hands to keep moving, quickly finishing my routine before stepping out of the bathroom. Ryan was stretched across the bed, leaning against the headboard with a book in his hands like he belonged there. The warm bedside lamp cast a soft glow across the room. He looked up the moment I stepped out. His face lit up with a gentle smile.

"There you are."

I walked toward the bed slowly, forcing my body to stay relaxed even though every instinct in me wanted to run. I watched enough movies about kidnappings. Stay calm. Play along. Give him what he wants until I can find a way out. Or until I could somehow contact Joe.

Joe's phone number was the only one I had memorized. If I could get access to a phone, any phone, I could call him. I just had to survive long enough to do it.

I climbed onto the bed carefully, pulling the blanket up as I lay down beside him. Ryan immediately wrapped his arms around me, pulling me against his chest like this was the most natural thing in the world.

"This is what I've always wanted," he murmured softly near my ear. "Just you and me. Together. I've imagined what our first night together would be like."

He kissed my forehead slowly, lingering there for a moment. Then his lips pressed against mine. I forced myself not to react. My body stayed still. My face stayed calm. But inside, I was screaming.

* * * * *

A month passed. The days blurred together in a strange routine that Ryan seemed determined to turn into something that resembled a normal life. Every morning, he woke up early and made breakfast in the kitchen downstairs. The smell of coffee and sizzling eggs would drift up the staircase and into the bedroom, pulling me from restless sleep. We would sit at the large wooden dining table that faced a wide window looking out over nothing but trees. Endless trees. The woods surrounded the house on all sides like a prison wall made of branches and leaves.

Ryan acted like we were simply a couple living together in a quiet cabin somewhere in the countryside. He talked about random things while we ate, news articles he had read, the weather, and what trails we might jog later that day. If someone had walked into the house and seen us at that table, they might have thought everything was perfectly normal.

But nothing about this was normal. Cameras sat quietly in the corners of the rooms, their small blinking lights reminding me that I was always being watched. The doors were locked at night. And Ryan never went anywhere without keeping an eye on me.

That morning, the sunlight streamed through the tall kitchen windows, casting long golden streaks across the wooden floor. Ryan folded the newspaper beside his plate and wiped his mouth with a napkin.

"Honey, I have to go into town today," he said casually. "We need groceries."

I looked up from my coffee. The word *town* immediately caught my attention.

"Can I come with you?" I asked carefully.

Ryan's eyes narrowed slightly.

"I hate being here alone," I added, keeping my voice soft and vulnerable. The truth was I hated being trapped here. But I couldn't let him hear that. Ryan frowned and leaned back into his chair, studying me.

"No," he said after a moment. My stomach sank, but I did not give up.

"Please?" I begged gently. "You can tie my hands and feet if you want. I'll stay in the car the whole time. I just… I don't want to be alone in this big house."

I lowered my eyes, playing the part, he seemed to want which was the obedient, dependent girlfriend. Ryan stared at me for a long moment. I could practically see the thoughts running through his mind as he weighed the risk. Then he sighed.

"Fine," he said finally. "You can go."

Relief flickered inside me, though I made sure not to show it.

"But," he added firmly, pointing a finger toward me, "I will tie your hands and feet."

I nodded quickly. "Okay."

Inside, my mind was already racing. Because leaving this house, even for a short trip, might finally give me the chance I had been waiting for.

* * * * *

The drive to town confirmed what I had feared the moment Ryan pulled the SUV out of the garage. We were deep in the middle of nowhere.

I sat in the back seat with my hands and feet zip-tied together, the plastic biting into my wrists every time the vehicle hit a bump in the road. The leather seats smelled faintly like pine cleaner and Ryan's cologne. I leaned my head against the window, pretending to watch the trees pass by lazily while secretly memorizing everything I could.

The gravel driveway crunched loudly under the tires as we left the property. Dust rose behind us in thick clouds, hanging in the air before slowly settling back onto the road. Tall pine trees crowded both sides of the narrow path, their branches reaching over the road like dark fingers. The forest looked like endless, thick green walls of trees, bushes, and tangled undergrowth. I couldn't see a single house, mailbox, or power line anywhere. Just trees.

The SUV rattled softly as Ryan drove over uneven patches of road. Every now and then the tires roll over loose stones, sending sharp cracking sounds up through the floorboards. The smell of damp earth drifted through the air vents, mixed with the faint scent of moss and wet bark.

I listened carefully. No traffic. No distant engines. No people. Only the low hum of the car engine and the occasional rustle of wind pushing through the treetops.

My stomach twisted.

We drove like that for nearly thirty minutes before the gravel road finally turned into pavement. The tires made a smooth humming sound once we hit the asphalt. A faded yellow line appeared in the center of the road.

Main road.

My heart beat a little faster. I glanced at the dashboard clock, quietly counting the minutes. Another thirty-minute drive passed before we reached a small town. Buildings began appearing along the road. First was a gas station, then a diner with a flickering neon sign, then a small grocery store with a faded red awning. I looked around carefully. People walked along the sidewalks. Cars filled the parking lots.

Every single license plate I saw read *Oregon*. So that confirmed it. We were in Oregon.

My eyes drifted toward the distant mountains barely visible through the morning haze, their peaks wrapped in low gray clouds. The air smelled different here, cooler, wetter, like rain and pine needles. Portland couldn't be far. If I could escape.

* * * * *

Three months later, I finally found the key to the deadbolt.

Ryan had left early that morning, like he had started doing more often lately. He said he needed to "go into work," though he never explained exactly what that meant. All I knew was that he would disappear for hours at a time, leaving me alone in the house while the cameras silently watched from their corners.

That morning the house was unusually quiet. No footsteps. No humming. No sound of Ryan moving around downstairs. Only the faint ticking of the wall clock in the kitchen and the distant rustling of wind outside as it pushed through the tall trees surrounding the property.

The smell of lemon cleaning spray hung in the air as I wiped down the kitchen counters. Ryan liked the house spotlessly clean, and I learned quickly that keeping the place clean made him calmer. The rag in my hand was damp and cool against my fingers as I ran it across the smooth granite countertop.

Sunlight streamed through the tall kitchen windows, warming the wooden floors beneath my bare feet. Outside, the forest swayed slowly in the breeze, branches whispering against one another like quiet conversations I couldn't quite hear.

My stomach growled softly. I had been cleaning all morning, sweeping the floors, wiping down the cabinets, organizing the pantry. It had become part of my routine. Cleaning kept my mind busy. It kept Ryan satisfied.

But mostly, it gave me a reason to search. Every drawer. Every cabinet. Every shelf. Every corner of this house.

I opened another cabinet above the counter, pretending to rearrange the bowls and plates stacked neatly inside. The wood creaked softly as the door swung open. My fingers brushed against something cold.

Metal.

I froze. Slowly, carefully, I reached behind the stack of mixing bowls sitting in the back corner of the cabinet. And there it was. A small brass key.

My heart began pounding so loudly I was sure the cameras could hear it.

The deadbolt key.

I had memorized that lock months ago, staring at it every time Ryan opened or closed the front door. I knew the exact shape of the keyhole. And this key matched it perfectly. My fingers trembled slightly as I turned it over in my palm. The metal felt cool and smooth against my skin.

Ryan was getting sloppy.

For months he had hidden every key in this house with obsessive care, locking them in drawers, keeping them in his pockets, moving them to different places every few days. But lately he became comfortable. Too comfortable. He thought I had accepted my place here. He thought I had given up.

But I hadn't.

Not even close. I slid the key back exactly where I found it and carefully pushed the bowls back into place, forcing my breathing to slow. My escape wasn't today. But now… Now I finally have a way out.

* * * * *

That night, Ryan came home furious. I had already told him earlier that evening that I was going to retire to bed early. My body felt weak and heavy all day, like a cold was creeping through my bones. I had barely touched my dinner and the smell of the soup I made for us had turned my stomach. After cleaning the kitchen, I curled up on the couch in the living room with a blanket, hoping the warmth might help settle the nausea.

The living room was dim except for the soft yellow glow of the floor lamp beside the couch. Outside the large windows, the forest was dark and silent, the tall trees swaying slightly in the cold night wind. The faint rustling of leaves and branches brushing against each other was the only sound in the quiet house.

Then the front door slammed. The sudden bang echoed through the house, rattling the picture frames on the walls.

Ryan.

The heavy sound of his boots stomped across the hardwood floors. His footsteps were fast and uneven as he moved through the kitchen and into the living room. The sharp smell of alcohol hit my nose before I even saw him.

I sat up slowly, pulling the blanket off my lap.

Ryan was pacing back and forth across the living room like a caged animal. His chest rose and fell rapidly with each breath, and his hands kept clenching and unclenching at his sides. His face was flushed red and his hair looked disheveled like he had been running his fingers through it repeatedly.

I did not know what had happened while he was out. But something had clearly pushed him over the edge.

"Ryan…?" I started carefully. Before I could finish, he turned toward me.

"You do not get to say no to me!" he screamed. The force of his voice made my heart jump. Then his hand struck my face. The sharp crack of skin hitting skin filled the room, louder than anything else in the house.

My head snapped to the side. Pain exploded across my cheek, hot and throbbing. My ears rang and my vision blurred for a moment as tears instantly filled my eyes. The metallic taste of blood spread across my tongue where my teeth had cut the inside of my lip.

"I only said I felt sick," I whispered, my voice shaking. My stomach still churned and the room spun slightly as I tried to steady myself against the arm of the couch. But Ryan did not care about that. Ryan never cared about that. Ryan only cared about himself.

The house had gone quiet after his outburst. Ryan had stormed off into the kitchen, leaving me sitting on the living room floor with my cheek still burning from the slap. The air felt heavy and tense, like the entire house was holding its breath. I stayed where I was for a while, listening.

Cabinets opening. The refrigerator door creaking. Glass clinking.

Ryan had never touched alcohol before, not once in the months I had been trapped here. He always claimed he did not need it, that he had "perfect control" over himself.

But tonight was different. The smell hit my nose before I even saw him again. Whiskey. Strong and bitter.

When I peeked toward the kitchen, I saw him leaning against the counter with a dark glass bottle in his hand. The amber liquid sloshed inside as he tilted it back and took a long drink straight from the bottle. No glass. No hesitation. Just gulp after gulp.

The sharp scent of alcohol slowly filled the house, mixing with the faint smell of wood and cleaning supplies. The sound of the bottle knocking against the counter echoed each time he slammed it down before lifting it again.

Ryan paced between the kitchen and the living room, drinking like a man possessed. His footsteps were uneven now, heavier than before. Every few minutes he would mutter something under his breath or run his hands through his hair like he was trying to shake something out of his head.

Then he grabbed another bottle from the cabinet. My heart began to pound. Bottle after bottle. He was unraveling.

His movements grew slower, less controlled. His shoulders sagged slightly as the alcohol began to take hold of him. When he stumbled into the living room again, I noticed something that made my breath catch.

His keys. They were still clipped to the loop of his pants.

Ryan always hid the keys the moment he came home. Every time. Without fail. Sometimes he tucked them into the top kitchen cabinet, sometimes into a drawer in the mudroom, sometimes into the pocket of a jacket in the closet.

But tonight… He had forgotten.

The small metal keychain clinked softly against his belt every time he moved. I could even hear the faint jingle of the keys over the quiet hum of the refrigerator and the whisper of wind outside the windows.

My pulse started racing so loudly I could hear it in my ears. This was the first mistake he had made in months. My fingers curled slowly against the floor as I forced myself to stay calm, to breathe slowly, to think.

Because this… This was my chance.

The living room lights were dim, casting long shadows across the hardwood floor. The only real light came from the small lamp beside the couch and the glow from the kitchen behind him. Outside the tall windows, the forest had turned pitch black, and the wind rustled faintly through the trees like whispers moving through the night.

Ryan sat slouched on the couch, his shirt half unbuttoned and his hair messy from running his hands through it. The strong smell of whiskey hung heavily in the air, almost burning my nose. Two empty bottles sat on the coffee table and a third dangled loosely from his hand.

His eyes were glassy. Unfocused. Perfect.

I forced my breathing to stay slow and steady as I stepped closer.

"Can I… help you relax?" I asked softly.

Ryan looked up at me, blinking slowly like it took effort for him to focus. Then he leaned back against the couch cushions, spreading his legs slightly.

"Fuck," he muttered. The sound of the word slurred together, thick with alcohol.

I knelt in front of him, trying to ignore the sour smell of whiskey in his breath. My fingers trembled slightly as I reached for the button on his pants.

Stay calm. Don't rush.

The room felt unbearably quiet except for the soft hum of the refrigerator in the kitchen and Ryan's uneven breathing above me. As I pulled his pants down, my hands slid into his pockets. Metal. Cold and solid against my fingertips.

The keys.

My heart slammed violently against my ribs. For a moment I was terrified he would feel my hands shaking or notice the sudden stiffness in my movements. But Ryan did not react. His head had already fallen back against the couch cushion, his eyes half closed as the alcohol dragged him deeper into a haze.

Slowly… carefully… I pulled the keys from his pocket. The faint jingle of metal sounded louder than thunder in my ears, but Ryan did not stir. I slipped them into my own pocket.

Ryan exhaled heavily and slumped further into the couch, his body going limp. Within minutes, his breathing grew deep and slow. The whiskey had finally knocked him out.

Drunk. Unconscious.

I stayed there for several seconds, barely breathing, watching him closely to make sure he would not wake up. Then I stood slowly. My legs felt weak, but adrenaline pushed me forward.

I had to move now. Before he woke up. I walked quietly to the closet and grabbed the metal chains he used to secure me to the bed. The cold metal links clinked softly in my hands as I carried them upstairs. Each step up the staircase creaked under my weight, the old wood groaning faintly in the silence of the house. Ryan was still asleep when I returned.

"Ryan," I whispered gently, shaking his shoulder.

He groaned but did not wake fully.

"Come on," I murmured softly. "Let's go upstairs."

He mumbled something incoherent and stumbled to his feet when I pulled his arm over my shoulder. The smell of alcohol rolled off him in waves as I guided him slowly up the stairs, step by step. His boots dragged across the wood and his body leaned heavily against mine, forcing me to support most of his weight.

By the time we reached the bedroom, sweat had formed along the back of my neck. I guided him towards the bed.

"Lay down," I whispered. Ryan collapsed onto the mattress without resistance. His eyes were closed now. His breathing deep and heavy. I moved quickly.

My hands worked fast but carefully as I wrapped the chains around his wrists and secured them to the thick wooden bedposts. The metal scraped softly against the carved wood as I tightened the locks. Then his ankles. One chain. Then the other. I double-checked each lock, my fingers shaking slightly as adrenaline surged through my veins.

Ryan did not move. Did not stir. Did not wake. For the first time in months… He was the one trapped.

I grabbed my backpack. The fabric straps felt rough against my sweaty palms as I slung them over my shoulder. My hands were shaking so badly I had to stop for a second and force myself to breathe. In through my nose. Out through my mouth.

The house was silent. Too silent. For months every creak in this place had terrified me. Now the silence felt just as frightening. My ears strained for any sound from upstairs, any movement, any shifting of the chains.

Nothing. Only the faint hum of the refrigerator and the distant whisper of wind moving through the trees outside.

Move. I hurried to the front door. The deadbolt stared back at me. For a second my fingers fumbled with the key. The metal scraped softly against the lock before sliding in. My heart pounded so violently I could feel it in my throat.

Click.

The sound echoed through the quiet house like a gunshot. I froze. Waiting. Listening. Still nothing.

Ryan did not wake up yet.

A rush of adrenaline shot through my body. I pulled the door open and stepped outside.

The cold night air hit my face instantly, sharp and damp with the smell of pine and wet earth. It felt like the first real breath I had taken in months. My lungs filled so deeply it almost hurt. The forest around the house was pitch black. Tall trees towered over the property, their branches swaying gently in the wind. Somewhere in the distance an owl hooted, the sound echoing through the woods.

For a moment fear gripped me. What if he woke up? What if he broke the chains? What if he was already coming down the stairs?

My stomach twisted violently.

Move. I forced my legs forward and ran to the garage. The concrete floor was cold under my bare feet as I slipped inside. The smell of motor oil and gasoline filled the air. My fingers trembled as I pressed the garage door button.

The heavy door groaned as it slowly lifted. Every second felt like an eternity. Then I jumped into the SUV. The leather seat was cool beneath me and the familiar smell of the car surrounded me again. My hands shook as I shoved the key into the ignition.

Please start.

Please start.

The engine roared to life instantly. Relief slammed into me so hard I nearly started crying. I threw the car into reverse and backed out of the garage, gravel crunching loudly under the tires. My headlights cut through the darkness, illuminating the long dirt driveway stretching out toward the forest.

My hands tightened around the steering wheel as I sped down the road. Branches whipped past the windows. Dust rose behind the car in thick clouds. My heart raced with a strange mix of fear and excitement that made my chest feel tight.

I was really leaving. After months of planning. Months of pretending. Months of waiting. I reached the main road and finally allowed myself to breathe again. The tires hummed smoothly on the pavement as I grabbed Ryan's phone from the passenger seat and opened the GPS. My fingers hovered above the screen for only a second before I typed one word.

Portland.

The route appeared instantly. Just over an hour away. I stared at the glowing map as the road stretched out ahead of me. My chest filled with something I hadn't felt in a long time. Hope. Freedom.

The drive felt endless. My hands gripped the steering wheel so tightly my knuckles turned white. The dark road stretched ahead of me like a tunnel cutting through the forest. The headlights of the SUV carved two pale beams into the darkness, illuminating twisting pavement, towering trees, and the occasional reflective road sign flashing past.

Every few seconds I glanced into the rearview mirror. My heart jumped every time I saw a pair of headlights in the distance.

Is that him?

My stomach twisted with fear. Ryan could wake up at any moment. He could break the chains. He could find the spare keys. He could be chasing me right now. The thought made my chest tighten until it hurt to breathe.

The smell of pine drifted in through the vents, mixed with the faint scent of leather from the seats. The steady hum of the engine vibrated beneath my feet, and the tires made a soft whispering sound as they rolled across the pavement. But my ears strained past those sounds. Listening. Waiting. Expecting to hear another engine racing up behind me.

My eyes kept flicking between the road and the rearview mirror. Every shadow on the road made my pulse spike. Every passing car made me grip the wheel harder.

Minutes felt like hours.

The dark forest refused to end.

My shoulders ached from the tension of holding my body so rigid. My throat was dry, and the taste of fear sat bitter on my tongue. Then suddenly…Lights.

At first, they were faint like tiny specks glowing in the distance like stars on the horizon. My breath caught in my chest. City lights.

As I drove closer, the darkness slowly gave way to the soft glow of streetlamps and traffic signals. Buildings began appearing along the road. Cars filled the lanes around me. Neon signs flickered in storefront windows.

Civilization.

The sight of it made my vision blur with sudden tears. I was actually going to make it. But even as relief washed through me, the fear never left. My eyes still kept darting in the rearview mirror. What if he was already behind me? What if he was watching me right now? The GPS guided me through several turns until a large, illuminated sign appeared ahead.

Adventist Health Hospital.

My chest tightened with overwhelming relief. I pulled into the emergency entrance, the tires screeching slightly as I braked harder than I meant to. Bright white hospital lights flooded the parking area, making my eyes sting after hours of darkness.

The engine was still running when I shoved the door open and stumbled out of the SUV. The cool night air hit my skin, carrying the faint smell of disinfectant drifting from the hospital entrance. My legs felt weak and unsteady as I forced myself toward the sliding doors.

Inside, everything smelled clean and sterile. Bright fluorescent lights buzzed softly overhead. The polished floors reflected the harsh white light as my footsteps echoed down the hallway. A nurse behind the front desk looked up just as I reached the counter.

I opened my mouth to speak. But the room began spinning. The lights blurred. My legs gave out. Then everything went black.

* * * * *

I wiped the tears from my face as the room fell silent. The steady *beep... beep... beep* of the heart monitor beside the hospital bed was the only sound breaking the quiet. The soft hum of the air conditioner filled the space, pushing cool air across my damp cheeks. The room smelled faintly of antiseptic and fresh linens, that sterile hospital scent that seemed to cling to everything.

All eyes were on me.

Xavier sat beside the bed; his hand wrapped tightly around mine. His thumb slowly brushed across my knuckles as if trying to calm me without interrupting. Joe stood near the foot of the bed, his arms crossed tightly over his chest, his jaw clenched so hard the muscles in his face twitched. Bruce leaned against the wall near the window, his expression unreadable but his eyes sharp and focused.

No one spoke. They were waiting. I took a shaky breath and forced myself to continue.

"When I woke up," I said quietly, my voice rough from crying, "two police officers were waiting to speak with me."

The memory flashed through my mind, the harsh hospital lights, the stiff plastic chair beside my bed, the serious expressions on the officers' faces.

"They searched the property," I continued, staring down at the blanket covering my lap. "But Ryan had already disappeared."

The room remained silent.

"My parents and Joe came to Portland," I said, swallowing the lump in my throat. "They moved me back home after I was released from the hospital."

I could still remember my mother's arms wrapped around me in the hospital room, the way she had cried into my hair as if she would never let me go again.

"There was enough evidence to charge him," I continued slowly. "But his parents were too powerful."

Joe shifted slightly behind me, the faint sound of his shoes scraping the floor breaking the silence.

"My family settled with them," I said. The words felt bitter in my mouth. "Twenty million dollars and a ten-year restraining order."

Xavier's hand tightened slightly around mine. I felt my chest tighten again as the fear crept back in.

"My restraining order is expiring. The judge refused to renew it." My voice trembled slightly now. "So, six months ago…"

I paused, blinking away fresh tears as they blurred my vision.

"He started sending me notes."

The paper. The handwriting. The words that made my skin crawl every time I saw them.

"That's why I left Montana," I said, my voice barely above a whisper. "I thought New York would be safer. I thought that I could get lost in the amount of people here."

The city seemed like the perfect hiding place. Millions of people. Crowded streets. Anonymous faces. I had thought I could disappear there. I began crying again, the sobs escaping before I could stop them. My chest shook as the fear I had been carrying for years finally spilled out.

"But he found me anyway," I choked. "If he gets me again…"

The thought made my stomach twist violently. "I won't escape this time."

Before I could say anything else, Xavier pulled me into his arms. His embrace was warm and firm, his chest solid against my cheek. I could hear the steady rhythm of his heartbeat beneath my ear. His hand moved gently through my hair as if trying to soothe away the terror.

"Shhh," he whispered softly. His voice was calm, steady, reassuring. "I've got you."

His arms tightened slightly around me. "You're safe now."

Chapter 21

XAVIER

The moment the doctor cleared Chasity to travel, we headed straight to the airport. There was no discussion. No hesitation.

The hospital still smelled of antiseptic and rubbing alcohol as we wheeled her through the hallway toward the exit. The fluorescent lights buzzed overhead, reflecting off the polished floors as nurses and patients moved quietly around us. Chasity walked slowly beside me; her arm wrapped in a brace and her face still pale from the concussion. I stayed close enough that my shoulder brushed her every few steps. If she stumbled, I would catch her.

Barry met us outside the hospital door and opened the car door for Chasity. The cool Florida air hit my face as we stepped outside, carrying the faint scent of salt from the ocean and the distant rumble of traffic. The moment she settled into the back seat, I started making calls.

Barry drove. Tyler rode shotgun. Nick sat beside me in the back.

I had Barry go back to the hotel to retrieve our belongings while Tyler stayed with us at the airport. By the time we landed in New York, I had already arranged for two additional bodyguards to meet us on the tarmac.

Aimme had taken care of the rest. She had gone to Chasity's house, packed everything she could, and had it delivered to my condo before we even boarded the plane. Chasity was no longer safe in her own home.

No matter how advanced the alarm system I had installed was, it couldn't compete with the security in my own building. My condo tower had three layers of controlled access, biometric entry, twenty-four-hour security staff, and surveillance on every floor. No one entered or exited that building without me knowing. And that was exactly how it was going to stay.

A million thoughts raced through my mind as the jet climbed into the night sky. The quiet hum of the engines filled the cabin, vibrating softly through the leather seat beneath me. The faint scent of jet fuel drifted through the ventilation system, mixing with the smell of expensive cologne and the coffee Nick had poured himself earlier.

All this time… I had been thinking about myself. About my feelings. About how much I wanted her. Meanwhile Chasity had been living in fear every single day. Scared out of her mind that some psychopath was going to drag her back into that nightmare. My jaw clenched as anger burned through my chest. If I ever got my hands on that bastard…

I would tear him apart. Every bone. Every nerve. I wouldn't stop until he begged for mercy. I couldn't believe what that man had done to her.

Six months. Six fucking months he held her captive.

The thought made my stomach twist with rage. My fingers curled into fists on my lap as I stared out the dark window beside me. I will protect her. No matter what.

I knew the moment I saw her at Joe and Bruce's wedding. The second she walked down that aisle. She was the one. And I wasn't going to let some psycho destroy her life again.

"This is him." Nick held out his phone.

Ryan Weiss. The bastard.

I took the phone and stared at the screen. The photo showed a clean-cut man in a tailored suit, standing confidently in front of a corporate office building. He looked normal. Too normal. That calm smile made my blood boil.

Ryan Weiss. Second son of Charles and Cheryl Weiss. Weiss Technology. I knew the company. Charles Weiss built it from the ground up. A self-made billionaire. New money. Just like me.

But Cheryl Weiss… She came from old money. And old money meant influence. Connections. Powerful friends who could bury problems before they reached the courts.

I scrolled through the profile Nick had pulled up.

Ryan had two siblings. Steven Weiss, the older brother. Current CEO of Weiss Technology. Angelica Weiss, the younger sister. Corporate attorney. All of them looked polished. Successful. Perfect. But somewhere in that family… There was a monster.

I handed the phone back to Nick and rubbed a hand over my face. Nick squeezed my shoulder.

"Don't worry," he said quietly. "You're my brother from another mother. I'm in this with you."

He leaned back into his seat, stretching his legs out. I nodded once. That was all I needed to hear.

I turned my head toward the other side of the cabin. Joe and Bruce had already fallen asleep in their seats across from us. The moment the plane took off, exhaustion had taken over. Joe's head leaned against Bruce's shoulder while Bruce's arm rested loosely across his lap.

They had been through hell last night too. No sleep. Too much stress. They deserved the rest. Then my eyes drifted toward the private bedroom at the back of the jet.

Chasity was sleeping inside. The doctor had given her medication before we left, and the concussion still made her dizzy. When she laid down earlier, she fell asleep almost instantly. I could still picture her fragile expression in the hospital room. The fear in her eyes. The way her hands trembled when she talked about him.

Ryan Weiss.

I leaned back in my seat and stared at the closed bedroom door. And made myself a silent promise. If that man ever came near her again… He wouldn't leave alive.

*****

It had been three months since our trip to Florida. Three long, tense months.

Thanksgiving had already come and gone, and winter had started creeping into the city. The air outside had grown colder, the trees along the streets now bare and skeletal against the gray sky. Christmas lights had begun appearing in shop windows and along apartment balconies, but the festive mood that filled the city did not quite reach me.

Because there was still no news of Ryan. Not a single sighting. Not a single note. No emails. No messages. Nothing.

On the surface, it should have been a relief. But it wasn't. Silence from someone like him was worse than threats. It meant he was waiting. Watching. Planning. I knew men like him did not simply give up. Not after everything he had done to Chasity. Not after the notes. Not after showing himself to her in Florida.

If he went through all that trouble, there was no way he was just going to disappear. Which meant he was out there somewhere. And when he moved again… I needed to be ready.

I sat on the couch in the living room, the quiet hum of the city filtering faintly through the windows thirty stories above the street. The condo was warm and dimly lit, the soft glow of the lamps reflecting off the dark hard wood floors. A half-finished glass of whiskey rested on the coffee table in front of me, untouched.

I had been staring at the security monitor on the tablet beside me for the last twenty minutes, watching the camera feed from the building lobby and garage.

Just in case. Then the front door opened.

"I'm home!" Chasity's cheerful voice filled the condo as she stepped inside, her suitcase rolling behind her. Chris and Landon followed closely behind her, both of them still wearing their winter coats from the cold outside.

The moment Chasity saw me on the couch, her face lit up. The tension in my chest loosened instantly. She walked quickly across the living room and dropped onto the couch beside me.

"We're heading out, boss," Chris said with a casual wave. Landon gave me a quick nod before both men turned and headed back toward the door.

Kate had stayed behind in New York to spend Thanksgiving with her husband and son, so Landon had taken her place as part of Chasity's security team for the trip. They had flown to Montana with her so she could spend the holiday weekend with her family. The door closed behind them, leaving the condo quiet again.

"How was Montana?" I asked, wrapping my arm around her shoulders and pulling her gently into my lap. Her hair smelled faintly like cold winter air and shampoo as she leaned into me. Chasity beamed, clapping her hands excitedly.

"It was great!" she said, practically bouncing with excitement. "Betty and Josiah literally grew half a foot each. I swear they're going to be taller than me before they hit middle school."

Her voice softened a little.

"It was so hard to leave them." She sighed dramatically, leaning her head against my shoulder.

I chuckled softly. I knew how much she adored her niece and nephew. Anytime she talked about them, her whole face lit up in a way that made it impossible not to smile.

"How's everyone else doing?" I asked.

"They're all doing well," she said with a small shrug. "Everyone's still alive and kicking, I suppose."

Then she tilted her head up toward me. "How was your Thanksgiving?"

"It was good," I said. "Nice seeing everyone again."

I leaned back against the couch cushions. "Penny found out she's having another girl."

Chasity's eyes widened instantly.

"Aww! I'm so happy for them!" she exclaimed. "Girls are fun to dress up!"

I laughed. "Lily seems indifferent about it."

"Well, she's only one," she responded.

"That makes sense."

Then she stretched her arms over her head and stood up.

"I'm going to go shower and unpack," she said, grabbing the handle of her suitcase. "Otherwise, my suitcase will just sit in our closet for weeks."

She rolled it down the hallway toward the bedroom. I watched her disappear around the corner before leaning back onto the couch. For the first time all day, the tension in my chest eased a little. Then I picked up the remote and started flipping through channels on the TV. But my mind wasn't really on the screen.

It was still somewhere else. Somewhere darker. Waiting. Because I knew Ryan Weiss hadn't disappeared. And when he finally decided to move again… I intended to be ready for him.

Chapter 22

CHASITY

We had a bright fire burning beautifully in the fireplace. I sat on the couch staring at it in admiration. My favorite blanket was wrapped around my shoulders and in my hands was a huge cup of tea. The cute pair of cozy socks that my sister had gotten me for Christmas was on my feet.

It had been about four months already since I moved in with Xavier. I really missed my house, all the furniture that I picked out, and my quirky office. There had been so many moments that I had wanted to go there, but I was smarter than that. I wasn't going to put myself in a compromised situation. I've read too many romance books where the heroine put herself in unnecessary danger, and the hero barely saved her in the nick of time. But this was my life and there was no way in hell that I was going to risk my life. I still had a lot of things to live for.

I wondered what Xavier and Nick were doing in Xavier's office. They had been in there for quite some time. Maybe they were discussing their new resort in Colorado. I knew that Xavier had been stressed about it. He told me that there were some complications with getting everyone on board.

I did not want to worry about Xavier's business right now. It was supposed to be a relaxing evening. Slowly my mind drifted off to daydream about more relaxing things such as the beach. I wanted to go on vacation to the beach. Maybe I could talk Xavier into going to Cancun with me one of these days.

I imagined that we were relaxing in a cabana on a private beach. Only resort guests had access to this beach. The sky was blue with some fluffy clouds drifting around. There was a slight breeze that ruffled the white curtains hanging on the cabana. I could smell the saltiness of the ocean water as they crashed onto the beach. I was napping while Xavier checked emails on his iPad.

"What are you thinking about?" Xavier's question cleared away my daydream, and I was pulled back to reality. He bent down and kissed the crown of my head before plopping on the couch next to me. Nick plopped down on the loveseat to our right.

"The warm beaches of Cancun," I smiled as I leaned my head on Xavier's shoulder. He wrapped his arm around me and pulled me even closer.

Xavier chuckled. "The beaches of Cancun aren't all that because there's too many resorts and tourists. If you want, I can take you to my private beach in Mexico."

My head shot up quickly. "You have a private beach in Mexico?" I squinted at him. I did not believe him. This guy barely got out of his office. Why would he have a private beach somewhere?

Xavier nodded. "He does," Nick chimed in. "Our beach houses are right next to each other. You're so lucky I talked him into buying it when we were building our resort in Cancun."

"When was the last time you went to your beach house in Mexico?" I questioned Xavier.

"When I bought it eight years ago," he shrugged like it was no big deal.

I unwrapped my left hand from my cup of tea and playfully slapped his arm. "How could you have a beach house in Mexico and still spend your winters in this cold?"

He kissed my temple. "I was waiting for you. You'll be the first person that I take to my beach house," he smiled.

"You are so sweet," I kissed his cheek. "I have no idea how I got so lucky to have snagged you."

"Ew," Nick commented. "Gross. This is the reason why I'm not into the whole committed relationship stuff."

I turned towards Nick and stuck out my tongue at him as Xavier laughed.

"Enough gross relationship stuff for tonight," Nick started to stand. "I'm heading out. I'll see you two at my parents' party this weekend," he said. Xavier and I got up and walked Nick to the door. I gave Nick a quick hug then the guys shook hands.

After locking up, we trotted back to the couch. "I have something for you," Xavier said as he picked up a jewelry box from the end table. I had no idea when it got there.

"We already exchanged Christmas gifts earlier today," I was confused. Why was Xavier giving me more stuff?

"Technically it's not a gift," he opened the jewelry box, and it was a beautiful jewelry set. It had a necklace, matching earrings, and a bracelet.

"Then what is it?" I looked up at him. Despite being together for almost a year now, I still couldn't get used to looking up at him. He was a foot taller than me.

"These are tracking devices. I wanted to make sure that I always knew where you were. It sounds a little crazy but until Ryan is gone from our lives completely, I want to take precautions," he explained.

I nodded. It made sense. I hadn't even thought about tracking devices. Xavier had thought of everything. "Thank you," I responded. "I'm so sorry that I dragged you into this mess. But I'm so thankful and grateful for you. You have been such a godsend. I don't know what I would have done without you," tears swelled up in my eyes.

"I'm happy to be in this mess with you and to protect you. I love you," Xavier kissed my forehead and pulled me into his arms. I wrapped my arms tightly around his abdomen as I rested my head on his chest.

Xavier pulled away from me and lifted my chin up with his hand. He leaned down and pressed his lips against mine. The moment our lips met, it sent shivers down my spine.

* * * * *

My jaw literally dropped as we walked into Warrington's mansion where they were hosting the New Year's Eve party.

Warm golden light spilled from massive crystal chandeliers overhead, making the entire foyer glow like something out of a movie. The air smelled faintly of expensive perfume, polished wood, and champagne. Somewhere deeper in the house, the soft sound of jazz music drifted through the rooms; smooth saxophones and piano notes blending with the low murmur of elegant conversation.

My eyes widened as I slowly turned my head, trying to take everything in. "Wow…"

The theme of the party was the 1920s, but every room seemed to interpret it differently. The foyer was decorated like a glamorous Gatsby entrance, black and gold everywhere, tall vases filled with white feathers, strings of pearls draped across marble tables. Beyond that, each room opened into something even more extravagant.

Waiters dressed as flapper girls and old-fashioned bartenders floated through the crowd carrying silver trays filled with champagne flutes and tiny appetizers. The scent of truffle oil, roasted meats, and buttery pastries drifted through the air, making my stomach rumble.

People laughed loudly around us, the sound of glasses clinking echoing across the marble floors. I swore I would never get used to how the upper class threw parties. This was on an entirely different level.

Xavier gently lifted my chin.

"Close your mouth," he whispered teasingly. I snapped my jaw shut and tried to regain some composure, though my eyes were still darting everywhere like a kid at Disneyland.

"Hun," I whispered to Xavier as I leaned closer to him, "can we check out all the rooms before you start mingling with your business associates?"

He laughed softly beside me. "Yes, we can."

Then he leaned down slightly. "And you don't have to whisper."

"I don't want people to know that I think it's kind of boring to mingle with the rich," I whispered anyway.

His shoulders shook with silent laughter. "I guess that's fair."

He gently placed his hand on the small of my back as we began strolling down the long hallway toward the main living room. Every step revealed something new.

One room looked like a vintage jazz club with velvet couches and a pianist playing softly in the corner. Another had towering champagne towers stacked like glass pyramids. The walls were lined with enormous paintings and mirrors framed in gold.

When we entered the main living room, my jaw almost dropped again. The entire space had been transformed into a ballroom. A large stage had been built against one wall where a live band played smooth background jazz. Couples in elegant dresses and tailored suits swayed slowly on the dance floor, the polished floor reflecting the soft glow of the chandeliers above. At the far end of the room was a massive open bar.

Xavier grabbed a glass of whiskey for himself and handed me a flute of champagne. The bubbles fizzed softly against the glass as I took a small sip.

"There you two are!" Nick suddenly appeared between us like a whirlwind and threw his arms over both of our shoulders. "I was starting to think you two ditched me!"

"Almost did," I said, pinching my thumb and pointer finger together. "But then I remembered you were the one who convinced Xavier to buy a beach house in Mexico."

I smiled sweetly. "I had to come save you."

Nick groaned dramatically. "You have no idea how many people are trying to set me up tonight."

He ran a hand through his hair. "Being one of the most eligible bachelors in New York is exhausting. Everyone's trying to introduce me to their daughters now that my best friend here is off the market."

I laughed.

"Just get a fake girlfriend," I suggested. "It happens all the time in my romance novels."

Nick paused. Then he slowly rubbed his chin. "You know what… That's actually genius."

He turned toward Xavier. "I need a fake girlfriend for events like this. My parents forbid me from hitting on women at their parties anyway."

Then he turned back toward me dramatically. He jerked his thumb toward Xavier. "Chasity, you're brilliant. How did this sucker convince you to date him?"

"Let go of my girlfriend," Xavier said, trying to pry Nick's arm off my shoulders.

Nick tightened his hold.

"Our girlfriend," he corrected. "I've done things for Chasity I've never done for any other woman."

He started counting on his fingers. "I bought her a house. Helped renovate it. Took her on vacation without being hungover the entire time."

He looked at Xavier proudly. "So technically she's my girlfriend too."

"Whatever," Xavier muttered, finally shoving Nick's arm off me.

I burst out laughing and slipped away from them. "You two are ridiculous."

Shaking my head, I headed down the hallway toward the restroom. After freshening up, I began searching for the guys again.

The party had grown louder while I was gone. The music had picked up slightly, and the smell of rich food filled the house, lobster bites, roasted duck, buttery pastries, and something sweet that smelled like caramel.

I finally spotted them in the dining room. They were standing with a small group of businessmen, casually snacking from a long buffet table. I leaned quietly against the doorframe and watched them for a moment. The sight made my heart flutter. Because the men I saw there were not the same playful idiots who teased each other on the couch at home.

Here… They were powerful. Confident. Respected. The room subtly revolved around them.

Xavier stood tall in a perfectly tailored Tom Ford suit, his posture relaxed but commanding. The soft lighting reflected off his polished Gucci loafers and the glass of whiskey in his hand. People leaned in when he spoke, listening carefully. He looked strong. Dominant. Irresistibly attractive.

But I knew the other side of him. The one who wore worn-out joggers and old Target t-shirts at home. The man who made me tea when I couldn't sleep. The man who held me when nightmares woke me up. My heart squeezed painfully with love.

Nick stood beside him, laughing at something one of the businessmen said. In the tabloids, Nick was the untouchable playboy bachelor. In the boardroom, he was ruthless enough to make seasoned executives sweat.

But at home with us… He was the guy who always showed up when we needed him. No questions asked. Just loyalty. Just family.

Xavier must have felt my eyes on him because suddenly he looked up. Our eyes locked across the room. I smiled softly and blew him a kiss. His serious business expression instantly melted into a warm smile that made my stomach flip. God, I loved that man.

After a few more minutes of conversation, the men finished their discussion and excused themselves. A few minutes later the three of us escaped the noise of the party and found refuge in Warrington's quiet study. Finally… A place where we could breathe.

* * * * *

The moment we stepped inside, the noise from the ballroom softened to a distant hum behind the thick wooden door. The room smelled faintly of leather, old books, and the warm smoky scent of the fireplace that crackled softly along the far wall. Dark wood shelves lined the room from floor to ceiling, filled with rows of neatly arranged books and framed photographs. A deep burgundy rug covered the floor, and several oversized leather armchairs were arranged around the fireplace like an invitation to sit and stay awhile.

I immediately gravitated toward the warmth. Xavier and Nick claimed the large couch near the center of the room; their heads already bent together in conversation about work before they had even fully sat down. Their voices were low and serious now, the playful banter from earlier replaced by the focused tone they used whenever business came up. Something about investors. Something about permits. Something about the Colorado resort.

I let their voices fade into the background as I curled up in one of the armchairs closest to the fireplace. The warmth seeped into my skin instantly, chasing away the chill that had clung to me from the cold outside. The firelight flickered across the room, painting everything in shades of gold and amber. I stretched my legs out slightly and sank deeper into the chair, letting out a quiet breath.

This was nice.

The faint sounds of jazz drifted through the walls from the ballroom, mixing with the soft crackle of the fire. Somewhere in the house, laughter erupted briefly before fading again.

I wrapped my arms loosely around myself and let my gaze wander to Xavier. He was leaning forward slightly, one elbow resting on his knee as he spoke to Nick. The soft firelight danced across his face, highlighting the sharp line of his jaw and the deep concentration in his eyes. Even when he was talking about work, he looked handsome. Dangerously handsome.

It still amazed me sometimes that he was mine. The powerful businessman who commanded boardrooms and built resorts across the country was also the man who made me tea when I couldn't sleep and wore worn-out joggers around the house.

A small smile crept onto my lips as I watched him.

Nick said something that made Xavier laugh quietly, and for a moment the serious expression dropped from his face. That familiar warmth returned to his eyes.

I leaned back into the chair, basking in the heat from the fire and the quiet comfort of the room. Then something caught my attention. Movement. It was subtle, just a flicker from the corner of my eye.

My head turned instinctively toward the doorway of the study. And there she was.

Maggie.

She stood just outside the doorway, half hidden in the dim hallway lighting. Her posture was stiff; her arms crossed tightly over her chest. Her expression was unmistakable. She was pouting.

Actually… pouting was being generous.

She looked furious. Her lips were pressed into a thin line, and her eyes were locked directly on Xavier. The firelight from the study illuminated just enough of her face to see the irritation radiating off her. But she did not step inside. She did not say anything. She did not even clear her throat to make her presence known. She just stood there for a moment, glaring into the room. Then she huffed.

The sound was quiet but dramatic enough that I almost laughed.

With an annoyed toss of her hair, she spun on her heel and stalked down the hallway. Her heels clicked sharply against the marble floor before the sound disappeared completely.

I blinked.

That was… strange. My gaze lingered on the empty doorway for another moment before I slowly turned back toward the room.

Nick and Xavier hadn't noticed a thing. They were still deep in conversation, completely absorbed in whatever complicated business issue they were discussing.

I tilted my head slightly. Maybe Maggie had finally given up. After all the years she had spent throwing herself at Xavier, maybe she had finally realized it wasn't going to happen.

That would certainly make life easier. A small shrug lifted my shoulders as I leaned back into the chair again. If Maggie had finally decided to move on… Well. That was probably the best New Year's gift I could ask for.

Chapter 23

XAVIER

"This is the ring." My finger rested lightly against the glass case as I pointed to the ring sitting beneath the bright showroom lights. The diamonds caught the light from every angle, scattering tiny sparks of white brilliance across the velvet display.

The sales representative's face lit up immediately. "Excellent choice, sir."

With practiced elegance, he unlocked the display case and carefully lifted the ring from its black velvet slot. He held it between two gloved fingers and extended it toward me.

The diamond was stunning. A princess-cut stone sat proudly at the center of a sleek silver band. Smaller diamonds were embedded all the way around the band like a halo of tiny stars, catching the light with every subtle movement.

I took the ring gently between my fingers. It was surprisingly light. But the meaning behind it felt heavy in the best possible way. I slowly rotated it under the light, watching the diamond flash with every small shift of my hand.

A warm surge of excitement rushed through my chest. A slow smile spread across my face before I could stop it.

This was it.

The ring.

The ring I was going to use to ask Chasity to marry me.

Just thinking about it made my heart pound. For the first time in my life, everything felt clear.

Chasity was not just someone I loved. She was the person I wanted to build my life with. The person I wanted to come home to every night. The person I wanted beside me when I was old and gray. The thought of losing her made my chest tighten. And the thought of spending the rest of my life with her… It made me feel something dangerously close to happiness.

"So…" Nick's voice broke into my thoughts as his hand clapped heavily against my shoulder.

"Are you going to buy it," he leaned closer to the glass case, "or are you just going to keep staring at it like a weirdo?"

He walked around me and started inspecting the other rings like this was just another casual shopping trip. I turned and gave him a flat look. "Of course I'm going to buy it."

I handed the ring back to the sales rep along with my credit card. His grin widened instantly. "Wonderful, sir."

He disappeared into the back of the store with the efficiency of someone who had done this a thousand times before.

Nick leaned against the glass counter beside me.

"You realize," he said casually, "that this is the moment where your life officially ends."

I rolled my eyes. "My life isn't ending."

Nick smirked.

"It's just beginning in a very different direction."

A few minutes later the sales rep returned with a small box nestled inside a white shopping bag. The bag was crisp and elegant. It was tied neatly with a black ribbon. He placed several documents in front of me.

"Just a few signatures here, sir."

I barely glanced at them. My name moved quickly across the page. When I handed the papers back, the small blue box suddenly felt like the most important object in the world.

The cold New York air hit my face the moment we stepped outside the jewelry store. Winter had settled deep into the city. The wind carried the smell of snow, car exhaust, and roasted chestnuts from a street vendor down the block. People rushed past bundled in coats and scarves, their breath visible in the freezing air.

I took a deep breath. If my reputation wasn't on the line, I probably would have been jumping up and down on the sidewalk like an idiot. Instead, I settled for a massive grin.

Nick noticed immediately. He placed a hand on my shoulder and shook his head slowly as we started walking down the busy street. "You're ridiculous."

We stopped at a small restaurant a few blocks away and slid into a booth. Nick took a long sip of his Coke before casually dropping the worst sentence imaginable.

"I hope Chasity doesn't leave you at the altar."

I glared at him.

"What?" He lifted his eyebrows innocently. "She's too good for you, man."

He took another sip. "I wouldn't be surprised if she wakes up tomorrow and realizes it."

I rolled my eyes. "Whose side are you on anyway?"

"Hers, duh," he replied instantly and leaned back into the booth. "Duh. I thought that was obvious."

Then his expression softened slightly. I looked down at the bag sitting beside me. The ring inside felt like it was glowing through the box.

"I won't," I said quietly. Because I meant it. The proposal had already been planned for months. Every detail. Every step. But life had thrown a wrench into everything. That wrench had a name.

Ryan Weiss.

Just thinking about the man made my jaw tighten. It had been months since Chasity last heard from him. Months of silence. But I did not trust silence. Not from someone like him.

So, while he had been quiet, I had been preparing. Security upgrades. Additional guards. Private surveillance. Every possible layer of protection I could add to Chasity's life. Because I refused to let that man ruin our future.

I refused to let Chasity live her life in fear. She deserved peace. She deserved happiness. She deserved the life she had always dreamed of. And I intended to give it to her.

After my upcoming trip to Colorado to meet Elliot Lancaster about the resort project, I was finally going to put everything into motion.

First step. Ask her parents for their blessing. My mom had already given me her blessing months ago when I told her I planned to marry Chasity. She had nearly cried on the phone.

Then came the second step. Fly both of our families to Montana. I would tell Chasity it was simply time for our families to finally meet properly.

Nick had already scouted the perfect place. A quiet hiking trail overlooking the mountains. Wide open sky. Snow-dusted peaks in the distance. The kind of place that looked like something straight out of a dream. The perfect backdrop. The perfect moment.

I could already picture it. Chasity standing there with the wind brushing through her hair. Her cheeks were pink from the cold. Her bright eyes looking up at me in confusion when I dropped to one knee.

The thought made my chest tighten. I loved her more than I had ever loved anything in my life. And in a few weeks… If everything went right… Chasity would become my wife.

*****

"Babe, are you sure you have everything packed?" Chasity asked for what felt like the hundredth time as she dug through my duffle bag again. For the third time. I leaned against the edge of the bed with my arms crossed, watching her with an amused smile as she pulled out my toiletry bag, unzipped it, then inspected the contents like she was conducting a security screening at the airport.

The bedroom was filled with the soft glow of the late afternoon sun filtering through the tall windows of my condo. The faint sounds of the city drifted up from far below, car horns, distant chatter, the constant hum of New York moving at full speed.

Meanwhile, Chasity was standing in the middle of the room in her oversized sweater and fuzzy socks, completely focused on my duffle bag like the fate of the world depended on it.

"Yes," I said patiently. "I do."

She ignored me and kept digging. I pushed off the bed and walked over behind her, wrapping my arms around her waist and pulling her gently back against me. She let out a small giggle as her hands paused mid-search.

"You know," I murmured against her hair, "I'm only going to be gone for one night and one day, right?"

She twisted slightly in my arms so she could tilt her head up and look at me. Her big brown eyes studied me suspiciously.

I gestured toward the garment bag hanging neatly on the closet door. "My suit is right there."

Then I nudged the duffle bag with my foot. "And the bag just has pajamas and toiletries."

I leaned down and pressed a soft kiss to her forehead. She squinted at me like she did not entirely believe me.

"Yes, I know," she said slowly. "And I know that you're rich enough that if you forgot your toothbrush, you could just buy a new one wherever you're going."

She zipped the duffle bag shut and finally stood upright.

"But that's not the point," she added, pointing a finger at me. "The point is you should already have one packed."

I laughed.

"Or…" I shrugged casually, "I could just not brush my teeth."

"Ew!" Chasity's nose scrunched up instantly in pure disgust. She shoved my chest lightly. "Please do not do that. That is disgusting."

Her expression turned dramatic. She crossed her arms. "I'll probably hear about it on TMZ the next morning."

She raised her voice into a mock news anchor tone.

"*Billionaire businessman Xavier Sterling skips brushing his teeth before major business meeting.*"

I chuckled.

"You know how they occasionally like to follow you around," she added.

I leaned down and kissed the tip of her nose. "I'm boring now."

She huffed. "You are not boring."

"Yes, I am," I said, smiling. "I go to work, come home, and hang out with my girlfriend. That's the life."

Her cheeks turned slightly pink at the word *girlfriend.* I gently nudged the duffle bag closed with my foot.

"Never mind the bag," I said softly. "We need to focus on the important stuff before I leave."

Her eyes narrowed playfully. "And what's that?"

Instead of answering, I leaned down and pressed my lips against her lips. She made a surprised little sound against my mouth before melting into the kiss. Her hands slid up my chest and around my neck as she leaned into me. The kiss started slow. Soft. But it quickly deepened.

Chasity laughed quietly when I pulled her closer.

"You're going to miss me that much?" she teased.

"Obviously," I murmured. "You're my favorite person."

Her eyes softened. "Good answer."

"But if you forget something and come home smelling like airplane breath…" She poked my chest then waved a warning finger at me. "You're sleeping on the couch."

I grinned. "Worth the risk."

She rolled her eyes, but the smile on her face gave her away. She was going to miss me too.

Chapter 24

CHASITY

My heels clicked sharply against the hardwood floors in the foyer as I stepped into the condo. The familiar scent of polished wood, expensive candles, and faint cologne still lingering from Xavier filled the air. Normally it made the place feel warm and comforting.

Today it just made me tired.

Chris closed the front door behind us with a quiet thud while Kate moved ahead of me down the hallway, doing a quick sweep of the apartment like she always did. Their footsteps were soft but purposeful, the quiet choreography of security that had become part of my daily life.

Today was exhausting. Not the *I need a nap* kind of exhausting. My *soul has been wrung out like a sponge* kind.

One of my students had broken down in my office earlier that afternoon after I asked him why his grades had suddenly dropped. At first, he tried to brush it off like it was nothing, but within minutes he was crying so hard he could barely speak. His father had just been diagnosed with stage four lung cancer. Stage four. The prognosis wasn't good.

The memory made my chest tighten again as I kicked off my heels near the entryway.

We had talked through options for taking an academic break, but he refused. If he lost his scholarship, he couldn't afford to come back to school. So instead, I spent the next hour on the phone with the director trying to figure out how to reduce his workload without jeopardizing his funding.

And that had only been the *first* emotional bomb of the day. My second client had dropped an entirely different kind of disaster into my lap during session. Her partner had disappeared without warning. No note. No explanation. Just gone. She kept asking me what she had done wrong. Like love was a math problem we could solve if we just found the right formula.

I let out a heavy sigh as I crossed the living room and collapsed onto the couch like a rag doll. The cushions sank beneath me, and the quiet apartment wrapped around me like a blanket. My eyes slowly scanned the empty space. God, I wished Xavier was home. I wanted to curl up next to him on the couch, bury my face in his chest, and let him hold me until the emotional weight of the day melted away.

But he wasn't there. He was halfway to Colorado. Xavier and Nick had been struggling for weeks to get the final approvals for their mountain resort project. Elliot Lancaster had apparently heard about the delays and offered to help smooth things over since he was already vacationing nearby with his wife.

So, Xavier had flown out to meet him and the local officials. Which meant Nick had stayed behind. To babysit me. Lucky him.

I pulled my legs up onto the couch and wrapped my arms around them, resting my chin on my knees. The soft fabric of my sweater brushed against my cheek as I took a slow breath. Even with Chris and Kate in the apartment, the place felt quiet. Lonely.

Maybe I'd FaceTime my sister later. Seeing Betty and Josiah always made me feel better. Those two little gremlins had the magical ability to fix any bad day.

The intercom suddenly beeped, snapping me out of my thoughts. Chris walked over and answered it. It was the doorman letting us know the delivery guy had arrived with our food. Before leaving campus, we had ordered takeout so it would arrive around the same time we did. Chris told the doorman to send him up.

"I'm going to change really quick," I called toward the hallway. "Then I'll be out for dinner."

Kate gave me a thumbs-up.

I shuffled down the hallway toward the bedroom, already peeling off my sweater as I walked. The walk-in closet felt cool and quiet as I stepped inside. I swapped my clothes for leggings and an oversized T-shirt, relishing the soft fabric sliding over my tired skin. Just as I finished pulling my hair into a messy bun, my phone rang.

Xavier.

A smile instantly tugged at my lips. I answered immediately.

"Miss me already?" I teased.

"No, I don't."

I froze. That wasn't Xavier. I slowly pulled the phone away from my ear and stared at the screen. It was definitely his number.

"I'm sorry… who is this?" I asked cautiously.

The response was a shrill, hideous laugh that made my skin crawl. Not laughing. More like a screech. Recognition hit me instantly.

Maggie.

"Just the person Xavier is with right now," she said smugly. "He probably told you he had some boring work thing, but he's actually on a trip with *me*."

I blinked. Then I started laughing. Like actually laughing. Because wow. The desperation was strong with this one. I leaned against the closet shelf.

"Oh good," I said cheerfully. "I'm glad he finally took some time off. The poor man has been working himself to death."

I paused dramatically.

"Thanks for keeping him company."

Then I added sweetly,

"So… how does it feel being the side chick?"

Silence. Then—

"*I'm not the side chick!*" Maggie shrieked.

I pulled the phone away from my ear before my eardrum exploded. Yep. That hit a nerve. I smiled at myself.

"Really?" I said casually. I shrugged even though I knew that she couldn't see me. "Because I live in his condo, spend his money, and sleep in his bed every night. You just get whatever time he can sneak away from me. Sounds like a side chick to me."

"You bitch!" Maggie screamed.

I rolled my eyes.

"You think you're so tough?" she continued. Then her voice turned vicious. "Just wait until you see what Ryan has planned for you."

My entire body became cold.

Ryan.

My stomach dropped like an elevator with snapped cables.

"What?" I whispered.

But Maggie was already laughing again. "He's coming for you. And you can't hide."

My hands started shaking. Then the line went dead. I stared at the phone in my hand.

Ryan.

How did Maggie know Ryan? My brain exploded with questions. My whole body felt numb. I stumbled slightly but caught myself on the closet shelf.

No. No no no. This was bad. Really bad.

Nick.

I grabbed my phone and dialed him immediately. The line rang.

Once.

Twice.

Three times. My heart pounded louder with each ring.

"Hello?" Nick answered.

"Nick, I—" A hand suddenly clamped over my mouth and nose. The smell hit me first. Sharp. Chemical. My body went rigid. My phone slipped from my fingers and clattered to the floor. Darkness swallowed everything.

* * * * *

My eyelids felt impossibly heavy. Like someone had glued them shut. For a few long seconds I floated in a thick, hazy darkness where nothing quite made sense. My head throbbed dully, and a sour chemical taste lingered in the back of my throat. My lungs burned slightly each time I inhaled, like the air itself had turned stale.

Was I really this tired? I forced my eyes open. The room swam into focus slowly.

Ryan. He was sitting on the edge of the bed.

The moment I saw his face; every ounce of sleepiness vanished. My body snapped into full alert like a switch had flipped inside my brain. My heart slammed violently against my ribs.

NO.

I jerked my head around quickly, scanning the room. The air smelled faintly of dust, expensive furniture polish, and something damp, like a house that hadn't been lived in regularly. The bedroom was large, far too large to belong to a hotel. Dark wooden furniture sat neatly arranged around the room: a massive bed, a dresser, two nightstands, a tall wardrobe.

Everything looked expensive. But lifeless. Cold. There were no personal items. No photographs. No warmth. A house. Somewhere isolated. Just like before.

My stomach dropped. I tried to move, and that's when I felt it. The ropes. My wrists were bound tightly to the arms of a chair, the rough fibers digging painfully into my skin. My ankles were tied to the legs of the chair as well. The coarse rope scratched against my skin every time I shifted. My pulse pounded louder.

"What do you want, Ryan?" I asked, forcing my voice to stay steady.

He grinned. "It's been a long time."

Once upon a time, I had thought that smile was sweet. Innocent. Now it looked like the grin of a psychopath. Cold. Predatory.

"Does your fiancée know you're here?" I narrowed my eyes at him.

Ryan chuckled softly. "You've been keeping up with my life too, I see."

He stood up and walked toward the wall, leaning casually against it like we were just two old friends having a conversation. He crossed his arms and studied me with disturbing calm.

"She's in Vegas," he said. "Bachelorette week."

I tilted my head slowly.

"How do you expect to keep me a secret from her?"

He shrugged like it was the most normal thing in the world. "Same way I've been doing it for ten years."

My stomach twisted.

"I tell her I have business trips," he continued casually. His grin widened. "Then I fly out to see you. She doesn't ask questions as long as her credit cards keep working."

A wave of disgust rolled through me.

"Wow," I said dryly. I shook my head slightly. "How incredibly predictable. So, your fiancée is one of those."

Ryan laughed.

"It works for both of us," he said. He shrugged again. "She keeps the image perfect. I keep her lifestyle funded. Win-win."

I stared at him. "So, you've been stalking me for ten years?"

"Enough catching up." Ryan pushed himself off the wall. My muscles tightened. He walked toward me slowly. "I've missed you."

He leaned down. His lips were aiming at my forehead. I turned my head sharply away. His hand shot out instantly, gripping my jaw and forcing my face back toward him. The smile vanished from his face. The first slap hit before I even realized what was happening.

CRACK.

My head snapped sideways. The sound echoed in the room. Before my brain could catch up—

CRACK.

The second slap came with his backhand. Pain exploded across my face. The metallic taste of blood filled my mouth.

"You do NOT turn away from me!" he screamed inches from my face.

I stared at him. My cheeks burned violently, the skin already swelling under the sting of his hands. My ears rang and my vision blurred for a moment. Tears flooded my eyes instantly. But I refused to let them fall. I refused to give him that satisfaction.

Ryan's hand suddenly fisted in my hair. Hard. Pain shot across my scalp as he yanked my head backward. I could feel strands of hair tearing free under the force. My neck strained painfully as he forced me to look directly into his face.

"I'm going to make you suffer for humiliating me," he whispered. His lips curled into a sick smile. "I'm going to have so much fun with you."

His mouth crashed against mine. My lips stayed tightly sealed. Rigid. He released my hair violently, shoving me backward into the chair. The ropes scraped harshly against my wrists as I struggled to steady myself. Ryan stepped back, breathing heavily.

"Oh, I have so many plans for you," he said. His eyes gleamed with excitement. "By the time I'm finished with you… No one will want you anymore."

His grin widened. Then he turned and walked out of the room. The door slammed behind him. Silence flooded the room.

My chest heaved. The tears I had been holding back finally broke free. They spilled down my face uncontrollably. Hot. Endless. My entire body trembled. I was terrified. Not the nervous kind of fear. The deep, raw kind that lived in your bones.

Xavier.

He was in Colorado. He did not even know I was gone. My parents. The thought of them hearing the news made my stomach twist painfully. I had been so careful. So cautious. I had never gone anywhere without Chris and Kate. Work. Home. The occasional outing with Xavier. That was it.

How had Ryan still managed to get me? How had he gotten past everything? My shoulders shook as quiet sobs escaped my chest. I couldn't do this again. The first time had nearly broken me. The months of abuse. The constant fear. The nights spent wondering if I would even survive.

It had taken years of therapy just to feel like myself again. Just to feel safe enough to let someone touch me. Just to love Xavier without flinching. And now…

Now it was starting all over again. The thought made my stomach churn. If he tortured me again… If I had to live through that again… Death might actually be easier. And that realization terrified me even more.

Chapter 25

CHASITY

"Chasity, I know that this is hard. It hurts, but if we don't try then you'll be stuck in this cycle forever," the therapist said softly. Her voice was calm and steady, the kind of voice that was meant to soothe people who were falling apart. It wasn't working.

I shook my head quickly, tears streaming uncontrollably down my face. My chest felt tight and raw from crying. A crumpled tissue was clutched in my left hand while my other hand pressed against my chest as if I could somehow hold my heart together.

"I just want to forget it all!" My voice cracked, sounding thin and desperate even to my own ears. The therapist nodded slowly, her expression gentle.

"I know you do," she said quietly. She leaned forward slightly in her chair. "That's a very normal response to trauma. Your mind wants to protect you from the pain. But avoiding it doesn't make it go away."

Her words felt heavy in the quiet room.

"You won't understand now," she continued gently, "but one day you'll understand why we have to talk about it."

"You don't understand," I whispered hoarsely. My eyes squeezed shut as another wave of tears rolled down my cheeks. My shoulders trembled with the force of my sobbing.

"The things he did to me…" my voice broke again. "It was disgusting."

The therapist did not flinch.

"It was," she said firmly. "It was disgusting. It was inhumane. And it was despicable."

The validation should have helped. Instead, it made my chest ache even more. The room fell silent except for the sound of my crying.

The office smelled faintly of lavender from the small diffuser sitting on the bookshelf behind her. Soft instrumental music played quietly from a speaker somewhere in the corner, meant to create a peaceful atmosphere.

It felt painfully out of place against the storm raging inside my chest. The couch beneath me felt too soft, like I was sinking into it while the weight of my memories crushed me from above. My tears kept falling. Hot. Endless. My breathing became uneven as I tried to calm myself, but every time I thought I had control again another image flashed through my mind.

Ryan's face.

Ryan's voice.

Ryan's hands.

My stomach twisted violently. The therapist remained silent, allowing the moment to pass without interrupting. Eventually the tears slowed. My throat burned and my head throbbed from crying so hard. I wiped my face clumsily with another tissue before blowing my nose. The tissue box beside me was nearly empty now.

I glanced at the clock on the wall. The session was over. Again. Another hour gone. And we accomplished nothing. Again.

I had been seeing this therapist for three months. Three long months. Every session ended the same way.

I would walk in thinking maybe this time would be different. Maybe this time I will finally talk about everything without falling apart. But the moment the memories started… The tears came. Every time. And once they started, they wouldn't stop.

I wiped the last dampness from my cheeks, but my face still felt swollen and hot. Even though I was technically safe now, my mind refused to believe it. The nightmares still came every night.

Ryan's voice would echo through my dreams, pulling me right back into those dark rooms where I couldn't escape. I would wake up gasping for air, my heart racing like I had just run for miles.

I couldn't leave the house without looking over my shoulder. Every shadow felt like danger. Every stranger felt like a threat. If I saw someone who even slightly resembled him, my chest would tighten and the world would start spinning.

Panic attacks came without warning.

My appetite had disappeared completely. Food tasted like cardboard when I forced myself to eat. My clothes hung loosely on my body now after losing more than twenty pounds in just a few months.

Some days I did not even have the energy to get out of bed. I would lie there staring at the ceiling, feeling hollow. Empty. Like someone had carved out everything inside me and left nothing but pain.

Joe and Alexi tried so hard to help. They took turns staying with me, refusing to let me be alone. They would sit on the edge of the bed telling me stories about their day. Funny little things that normally would have made me laugh. But their voices felt distant. Like they were talking to someone else. Nothing they said stayed in my mind.

I was hollow. A shell of the person I used to be. And the only thing left inside me… Was pain.

* * * * *

Feet flat on the ground. Hands resting on my lap. Back straight against the couch. That's what the therapist always told me to do when things started getting overwhelming.

Ground yourself.

I focused on the feeling of the carpet beneath my shoes, the firmness of the couch cushion under my thighs, the soft fabric of the tissue still crumpled between my fingers. The room smelled faintly of lavender and clean linen, the same calming scent that filled the office every time I came here.

It was supposed to make this easier. It did not. I drew in a deep breath through my nose. The air felt cold as it filled my lungs.

One.

Two.

Three.

Four.

Five.

I held it like she taught me. Then I slowly released it through my mouth. My chest trembled as the air left me.

"We met in freshman writing," I finally said, my voice sounding small in the quiet office. The therapist did not move. She just sat there across from me, hands folded loosely in her lap, giving me her full attention.

"Every day after class he would walk up to me," I continued. I stared down at my hands as the memory unfolded in my mind. "He'd ask if I wanted to study with him… grab lunch… grab coffee. I rejected him every time."

My fingers tightened around the tissue. A shaky breath left my lungs.

"But he was persistent. He offered to help carry my textbooks from class to class."

At the time, it had seemed harmless. Friendly. Normal. My voice dropped lower.

"I thought he was just being nice. Joe told me I should tell him clearly that I wasn't interested."

My throat tightened.

"So, I did."

I swallowed hard.

"And a few weeks later…"

My voice faltered.

"…he kidnapped me."

The word hung in the air between us. Kidnapped. It still felt unreal even though I said it out loud.

"I don't know for sure," I whispered, "but I think he had been planning it for months."

The therapist's expression did not change. Her calm presence filled the space, waiting patiently while I struggled through the memory.

"He took me to a farm in Oregon."

My hands started to tremble slightly.

"I was held captive for six months."

The number made my stomach twist. Six months. Half a year.

"Those six months were the worst days of my life."

I paused, forcing another deep breath into my lungs. The air felt thicker now, harder to pull in. The therapist remained silent. Waiting. She knew pushing me would only make it worse. It had taken us an entire year to reach this point.

A whole year before I could say these words without completely shutting down. Besides the police officers who took my statement, she was the first person I had ever told the full story to. I couldn't bring myself to tell my parents. Or Joe. The shame was too heavy.

"Ryan chained me to the bed whenever he left the property," I continued quietly. My fingers dug into the tissue. "I couldn't move. I couldn't go anywhere."

The memories started pushing harder now, forcing their way to the surface. My chest tightened.

"He raped me every day."

The word scraped painfully out of my throat.

"If I was lucky…"

My lips trembled.

"…it was only once."

My breathing became uneven.

"If I wasn't lucky…"

My shoulders started to shake.

"…it was multiple times."

The therapist leaned forward slightly but did not interrupt.

"My body was covered in bruises. He slapped me. Hit me. Kicked me."

I could see them again. Purple. Blue. Yellow. Everywhere. My voice cracked.

"Sometimes it was because I didn't answer fast enough."

Another tear slipped down my cheek.

"Sometimes because I walked too slow."

Another one followed.

"Sometimes because I didn't look him in the eye."

My chest heaved.

"Or some other stupid reason he made up."

My vision blurred as the tears filled my eyes again.

"I never raised my voice," I whispered. "I never fought him."

The words tasted bitter in my mouth.

"I just… let him do it."

My lips quivered violently now.

"I hate myself for that."

The words burst out before I could stop them.

"I hate the fact that I didn't fight back!"

My voice cracked, the emotion finally spilling over.

"I just let him do those disgusting things to me!"

The tears finally broke free. Hot. Uncontrollable. My shoulders began to shake as sobs ripped through my chest. My breath came in sharp, uneven gasps as the emotions I had buried for so long clawed their way to the surface. Across from me, the therapist's voice remained soft and steady.

"Don't fight the tears," she said gently. "Let them come."

Another sob escaped my throat.

"It's part of the process."

I covered my face with my hands as the tears fell harder. Fear. Shame. Anger. Disgust. Relief. All of it tangled together inside me, crashing against my chest like waves during a storm. For the first time in a long time… I was finally saying it out loud.

*****

"Imagine that you're with another woman who went through the same thing you did," my therapist said gently. "What would you say to her?"

Her voice was soft but steady, the same grounding tone she had used with me for nearly two years now. The office smelled faintly of lavender and tea leaves from the mug sitting on the table beside her chair. Afternoon sunlight filtered through the tall window behind her, warming the room in a quiet, comforting glow.

I closed my eyes and leaned back onto the couch. The fabric was soft against my shoulders, and I could feel the weight of the blanket draped across my lap. My breathing slowed as I inhaled deeply through my nose. The air felt cool. Clean. Then I slowly exhaled.

"You are brave," I said quietly. "You're a survivor. You were smart and planned an escape."

The words felt strange leaving my mouth. Almost unfamiliar. My therapist waited a moment before speaking again.

"Now," she said gently, "say that to nineteen-year-old Chasity Yang."

I bit down on my lower lip as the image began forming in my mind. Slowly. Reluctantly. I imagined standing in front of my younger self. She looked exactly the way I remembered.

Broken.

Her shoulders were slumped forward as if the weight of the world had been placed on them. Her eyes stared down at the ground, hollow and distant. Tear stains streaked across her cheeks, leaving faint salty trails on her skin. Her lips were dry and cracked. Her hair was tangled and oily, hanging lifelessly around her face. It hadn't been washed in days, maybe longer.

She looked so small. So fragile. The oversized gray T-shirt she wore was wrinkled and stretched out, clinging awkwardly to her thin frame. The black jogger sweatpants hung loosely around her hips. She hadn't changed clothes in a while. She hadn't cared enough to.

The sight of her made my chest ache. This was me. Or at least the girl I used to be. I stepped closer. The darkness around us was absolute. No walls. No ceiling. No sound. Just endless blackness stretching in every direction like we were floating in some quiet, empty universe. No one existed here except us. I slowly lifted my hands and placed them on her shoulders. Her body felt fragile under my palms.

"You are…" my voice trembled. I swallowed hard and took a deep breath. Tears began gathering behind my eyes. "You are brave."

My voice steadied.

"You're a survivor."

I squeezed her shoulders gently.

"You were smart. Smarter than any nineteen-year-old out there."

My chest tightened with emotion.

"You knew how to outsmart Ryan."

The words poured out in a rush.

"You planned. You waited. You escaped."

Tears slid down my cheeks now, warm against my skin.

My younger self slowly lifted her head. Her eyes met mine. For the first time, I saw something there that I had never allowed myself to see before.

Hope.

Tiny at first. Like a spark. But it was there. Color began bleeding slowly into the gray shirt she wore. At first, it was faint, like watercolor spreading across paper. Then the color deepened. Richer. Warmer. The gray fabric transformed into a flowing red dress that shimmered softly in the darkness. Her hair smoothed itself into long, shining strands, clean and brushed.

Her posture straightened. Her face lifted. It felt like watching a transformation. Like that moment in *Beauty and the Beast* when the spell finally breaks. Except this time…

The transformation wasn't happening to a beast. It was happening to me. The broken girl I had carried inside me for so long wasn't broken anymore. She was strong. Alive. Free. The realization rushed through my chest like a burst of light.

My eyes snapped open. I stared at my therapist, stunned. My mouth opened as a breath rushed out of my lungs. "What…"

I shook my head in disbelief.

"What just happened?"

The feeling in my body was overwhelming. The tight knot that had lived in my chest for years suddenly felt… less. The constant weight that had pressed on my shoulders for so long felt lighter. My heart raced as I started talking rapidly, my hands flying through the air as I tried to explain what I had just experienced.

"It was like… I saw her… and then she changed… and the color… and the dress… and…" I stopped myself mid-sentence, realizing I had been rambling like a lunatic.

My therapist smiled softly. "Chasity."

Her voice gently interrupted my spiraling thoughts. I finally fell silent.

"This," she said calmly, "is the beginning of your healing."

My breathing slowed as I listened.

"What happened," she continued, "was your brain's way of processing and releasing the trauma."

She leaned forward slightly.

"For the first time, you showed compassion to your younger self instead of blame."

Her words settled deep inside me.

"And that's powerful."

I sat there quietly. My chest felt lighter. Clearer. Like a door inside my mind had finally opened.

"For a long time," she said softly, "those memories controlled you."

She smiled.

"But today… your brain showed you something important."

I looked down at my hands resting in my lap.

"They don't have power over you anymore."

And for the first time in a very long time… I believed her.

Chapter 26

CHASITY

I did not know how much time had passed when Ryan woke me up with a slap across my face. The sharp sting exploded across my cheek, snapping me out of the heavy fog I had been drifting in. My head jerked to the side and a dull ring filled my ears.

For a moment I could not tell if it was night or day. The room was dark. Pitch black except for the faint gray light leaking through a window somewhere in the room. My eyes struggled to adjust as my vision slowly cleared.

Ryan was crouched in front of me. The smell of alcohol clung to him, sour and sharp as it filled the air around us. He did not say a word. He was untying the ropes around my wrists and ankles. The coarse rope scraped painfully against my skin as it loosened. My hands felt numb and stiff when the circulation started returning, pins and needles stabbing through my fingers.

Ryan suddenly grabbed my elbow and yanked me upward. "Get up."

My legs barely worked. My muscles were stiff and aching from being tied to the chair for so long. My body felt heavy, sluggish, like every bone inside me had been replaced with sand.

Ryan wasn't patient. He dragged me forward anyway. My bare feet scraped across the cold wooden floor as I stumbled after him. The house was silent except for the creaking floorboards beneath our weight and the pounding of my heart in my ears.

I did not dare ask where we were going. I did not want to know what kind of torture he had planned next.

Ryan pulled me down a hallway that smelled faintly of damp wood and stale air. The house felt empty, lifeless, like it had been abandoned long before we arrived. We reached the front door.

A thick winter jacket hung on a hook beside it. Ryan grabbed it and shoved it roughly onto my shoulders. The fabric was cold against my skin. The gesture confused me. Despite everything he had done… he still did not want me dead. Not yet. He still had plans for me. The thought made my stomach twist.

Ryan suddenly swung the door open. A blast of freezing air hit my face so hard it stole the breath from my lungs. The wind howled violently through the doorway, carrying the sharp scent of pine trees and snow. The cold burned my skin instantly. Ryan shoved me forward.

"Move."

I stumbled outside. Snow crunched under my feet as I struggled to keep my balance. The ground was uneven and slick beneath me, and the icy wind cut through the thin fabric of the jacket like knives.

Ryan slammed the door behind him. The darkness outside was deeper than the room had been. No lights. No houses. No sounds except the violent rustling of trees in the wind.

Ryan grabbed my elbow again and started dragging me away from the house. Toward the woods. My breath came out in short white puffs as the cold air clawed into my lungs. My fingers and toes were already starting to go numb. Confusion twisted inside my chest.

What was he doing? Why bring me outside? My heart began racing faster with every step. Was he going to kill me out here? The thought slammed into me so suddenly that my stomach was lurched.

The woods stretched ahead of us like a black wall of shadows. The tall pine trees swayed in the wind, their branches creaking softly as snow drifted down from above. The deeper we walked, the darker it became.

My mind raced. Was this it? Was this where he planned to bury me?

The cold seeped deeper into my bones with every step. Even with the jacket, the freezing wind bit painfully into my face. Fear spread through my chest like ice. I had no idea what Ryan was about to do. And somehow… That uncertainty terrified me even more than the pain.

Chapter 27

XAVIER

The moment Nick's voice exploded through the phone, something inside my chest snapped. "She's gone!"

The words did not even register at first.

Gone?

My mind refused to process it. I slowly moved the phone back toward my ear after pulling it away from the initial shock of his shout.

"Who?" I asked, my voice suddenly dry.

Nick took a breath at the other end of the line. I could hear movement behind him, doors slamming, people shouting, footsteps echoing through the condo.

"You have to come back," he said, his voice suddenly controlled, which only made it worse. "Chasity is gone."

Everything inside me went still. Completely still.

Nick continued speaking quickly. "She called me earlier. Her line suddenly went dead. Thank God I was already on my way over when she called. Chris and Kate were both knocked out cold when I got here."

The words slammed into my brain like hammer blows.

The security bodyguards were knocked out.

Chasity was gone.

My grip tightened around the phone until my knuckles turned white. I looked up slowly.

Barry was watching me. He already knew something was wrong.

"I'll be back soon," I said into the phone before hanging up. The words barely left my mouth before I turned to Barry. "Code black."

His posture changed instantly. No hesitation. No questions. He pulled his phone out immediately.

"Call Tristan," I added.

Barry nodded once. We had planned for this. For months we had prepared for the possibility that Ryan would eventually try something again. Layers of security. Tracking devices. Emergency response protocols. But planning for something and actually hearing that it had happened were two very different things.

My heart was pounding so hard I could feel it in my throat. I turned toward the cockpit. The pilot barely had time to greet me before I was already speaking.

"We're turning around."

He blinked.

"Sir, we're already halfway…"

"Turn the plane around." My voice was calm. Dead calm. The kind of calm that made people nervous.

The cockpit went silent for a moment. Then the pilot nodded and began communicating with air traffic control. Within minutes the jet blanked hard in the sky, the engines roaring as we turned back toward New York.

I paced the cabin like a caged animal. The jet smelled faintly of leather seats and jet fuel, but all I could taste was adrenaline. My hands trembled slightly as I dialed Aimme.

She answered immediately. "Xavier?"

"Chasity's been taken."

There was a brief pause. Not panic. Just calculation.

"I'll take the Colorado meeting," she said instantly. "Send me the briefing files and I'll be on the next flight."

I closed my eyes for a moment. Aimme truly was a godsend. "Thank you."

Next call. Elliot Lancaster. I explained the situation quickly and apologized for not having the meeting. Elliot did not hesitate.

"Family comes first," he said. "We'll get the council on board. Don't worry about that."

I hung up. Then the anger finally hit.

"How did he get in?" I shouted into the cabin.

No one answered. Because no one had the answer.

* * * * *

Six hours.

It had already been six hours since Chasity disappeared. Ryan had waited. Watched. Planned. He knew exactly when to strike. He waited until I left town. Until Chasity was vulnerable.

"Calm down!" Nick's voice came through the speaker as we were on the call. "Yelling won't help."

"I swear to God if he touches her—" My voice broke off. I did not even finish the sentence. Because if I did, I might lose control.

Tristan's voice suddenly cut into the call. "Well… I'll give the guy one thing."

My head snapped toward the speaker.

"He thought of everything."

"What does that mean?" I demanded.

"Explain later," Tristan replied casually, fingers clacking rapidly across keyboards. "Right now, you should focus on saving your woman. I found her."

Everything in the room froze.

"What?"

"Tracking devices," Tristan said. "The ones you put on her jewelry. They pinged about five hours upstate."

Five hours. My stomach dropped.

"I sent the coordinates to your phone."

My hands slid down my face as relief and dread collided inside my chest.

"Thanks."

"Don't mention it," Tristan said. "Now go get her. I'll deal with your system."

The moment the jet landed we did not even slow down. Barry and I practically sprinted through the terminal with the rest of my security team behind us. Cars were already waiting. Engines running. Weapons loaded. Forty-five minutes later we were racing through the snow-covered roads upstate.

* * * * *

The house appeared like a shadow in the middle of nowhere. Old. Dark. Isolated. Perfect for a psychopath.

"Check every nook and cranny!" I shouted as my team poured into the house. My gun was already in my hand as I moved from room to room. Kitchen. Empty. Living room. Empty. Bedroom. Empty. Frustration boiled inside my chest.

Eleven hours.

Eleven hours since Chasity had been taken. If he hurt, her… No. I pushed the thought away before it could finish forming.

Barry's voice echoed through the house. "Clear! No sign of them inside!"

My jaw clenched so hard it hurt.

Then one of the guards ran in. He pointed toward the back of the house. "Sir! Footprints in the snow!"

Fresh. Heading toward the woods. Maybe thirty minutes old. Every muscle in my body tense.

"Let's go get that bastard."

The team moved instantly. Outside the night air cut like knives through our jackets as snow crunched beneath our boots. A drone lifted into the sky with a soft mechanical whir, its heat sensors scanning the forest.

I followed the team deeper into the woods, tracking the prints through the snow. The forest was silent. Too silent. The only sounds were our breathing and the crunch of boots against ice. My heart hammered violently in my chest.

Please.

Please let her be alive.

There were still so many things I wanted to do with her. So many places I wanted to take her. God, I hadn't even proposed yet.

"Sir," Barry said quietly through the comm. "The drone picked up two heat signatures."

My pulse spiked. "Distance?"

"About a hundred meters ahead."

I tightened my grip on the gun. Ryan. And Chasity. We were close. Very close. And if that bastard had laid one finger on her…

Chapter 28

CHASITY

Did I just hear Xavier's voice?

The sound floated through the trees, faint but unmistakable. My heart lurched violently in my chest.

No… that couldn't be right. My brain must have been playing tricks on me. The cold had seeped so deeply into my bones that I could barely feel my fingers anymore. My toes were numb inside the thin shoes Ryan had dragged me outside in. Every breath burned as icy air clawed its way into my lungs. I had to be hallucinating.

Xavier was in Colorado. He was supposed to be meeting with Elliot Lancaster. There was no way he could have flown back already. Unless… A terrifying thought crawled into my mind. Unless I had been here for days. Panic surged through my chest so fast it made my stomach twist.

How long have I been gone?

Did they even know where I was?

Did Xavier think I had disappeared again?

The thought made tears sting the corners of my frozen eyes. I did not want to die out here. Not like this. Not before I got to live my life. Not before I got to love Xavier the way I wanted to. I hadn't even told him everything yet.

We talked about the future in quiet moments. The vacations. The family. The life we were supposed to build together. A lump rose painfully in my throat.

I don't want this to be the end.

"Fuck," Ryan muttered under his breath. The word snapped my attention back to him. I turned my head slightly. He had stopped walking. Completely still.

The wind rustled through the tall pine trees around us, carrying the sharp scent of snow and frozen earth. My ears rang from the cold and the pounding of my heartbeat.

Ryan looked tense. Like an animal deciding whether to run or fight.

Before I could react, he suddenly grabbed me. Hard. He yanked me backward against him, my back slamming into his chest. My breath rushed out of my lungs as his arm wrapped tightly around my neck.

My vision filled with blinding light. A beam from somewhere in the trees ahead cut through the darkness and hit my face directly. I squinted, unable to see anything but brightness. My heart pounded violently against my ribs.

Ryan's grip tightened around my throat as he raised his gun toward the light.

Shock flooded through my exhausted body. I barely moved. I barely breathed. My body had nothing left. I was freezing. My lips were dry and cracked. My stomach ached from hunger. My throat burned from thirst. I did not even have the strength to fight him.

"Don't come any closer or I'll kill her!" Ryan screamed into the darkness. His voice echoed through the trees, wild and frantic. The gun shook in his hand as he waved it toward the light.

Figures began emerging from the darkness. Shapes. People. My vision slowly adjusted enough for me to make out silhouettes moving closer. My heart jumped painfully. Then I saw him.

Xavier.

It was really him. Relief slammed into me so hard it almost knocked the air out of my lungs. He was here. He actually came. A sob caught in my throat. For a split second I felt something I hadn't felt since Ryan grabbed me in the closet. Hope.

"Ryan," Xavier said calmly. His voice was steady, controlled. "We don't want to hurt you."

My chest tightened painfully at the sound of his voice.

"Just let Chasity go."

Ryan let out a crazed laugh beside my ear.

"Let her go?" he sneered.

His arm tightened around my throat again.

"I will NEVER let you have her!"

His breath was hot and foul against my ear.

"She's mine!"

"Please…" My voice came out weak and hoarse. The cold had stripped all strength from it. "Please Ryan… let me go."

For a moment I thought maybe… Maybe he would. But Ryan only leaned closer to my ear.

"Never." His whisper was cold. His fingers dug into my shoulder. "You were mine first. And you'll always be mine."

My stomach twisted violently.

"If he knew the truth," Ryan continued softly, "if he knew everything that happened between us…"

His lips brushed my ear.

"He wouldn't even want you."

Pain stabbed through my chest. Because that fear… That horrible, ugly fear… Had lived inside me ever since Xavier came into my life.

What if he knew everything?

What if it made him look at me differently?

What if the broken pieces of mine were too much?

"I bet you never told him everything," Ryan whispered. "That's why he's doing this."

His voice turned possessive.

"You're mine."

His arm tightened around my neck again. His breath brushed my ear.

"No matter where you run. I'll always come for you."

"Let's negotiate," Barry's voice cut through the tension. Strong. Controlled. I could see him standing beside Xavier now. Other members of the security team spread out around them like silent shadows in the snow.

Ryan's body stiffened instantly.

"I will NOT negotiate!" he screamed. The gun jerked wildly in his hand. "You want her?"

His voice turned manic.

"Then come and get her!"

Everything slowed. Time stretched strangely.

Ryan suddenly shoved me forward. My body lurched out of his grip. My feet lost their balance in the deep snow. The world tilted sideways.

As I fell, I caught one last glimpse of Ryan. He was laughing. Actually laughing. Then… Gunshots. Loud. Sharp. They cracked through the forest like thunder.

Ryan's body jerked violently as the bullets hit him.

One.

Two.

Three.

His knees buckled. He collapsed into the snow. But I never hit the ground. For a moment my body kept falling. Weightless. Like I was floating. I was too afraid to open my eyes. Too afraid to see what came next. Darkness swallowed me whole.

Chapter 29

XAVIER

"Chasity!" I screamed as her body vanished into the darkness. The sound tore from my throat before my brain could even process what had just happened. One second, she had been there. The next… Gone.

"I need lights!" My voice came out hoarse and frantic. "I can't see her!"

I ran forward, boots slipping in the snow as I rushed past Ryan's lifeless body toward the edge where Chasity had disappeared. My lungs burned from the cold air slicing into them as I dropped to my knees at the edge of the cliff.

"Sir!" One of the guards grabbed my shoulder and swung his flashlight downward. The beam cut through the darkness below us. My stomach dropped.

"It's a cliff," the guard said grimly. "I don't know how deep it goes."

The world seemed to tilt. A cliff. She fell off a cliff.

"Call the helicopter!" I barked. My voice echoed sharply through the frozen forest. "Get it here ASAP! I need to find her!"

The team moved instantly. Radios crackled. Boots pounded across the snow. The forest filled with urgent movement and clipped commands. But I couldn't move. I just stood there at the edge, staring into the black void below. The wind whipped across the cliffside, biting against my face and stinging my eyes. My hands trembled as adrenaline coursed violently through my veins.

Someone radioed for the helicopter. Another guard checked Ryan's body. Others began pulling ropes from their packs, securing anchors to nearby trees before preparing to descend the cliff.

Everything was happening around me. Fast. Efficient. Professional. But all I heard was ringing. A high, shrill ringing inside my ears. Barry was talking to me, his mouth was moving, but I couldn't hear a single word. My brain refused to process anything except one thought.

Chasity.

She had to be okay. She had to be.

My heart slammed violently against my ribs, so hard it hurt. Every beat felt like it might burst through my chest. Fear swallowed everything else.

I closed my eyes for a split second, and suddenly images flooded my mind. The life we were supposed to have. The house I wanted to buy for us someday. Two stories. White siding. A wraparound porch. A white picket fence.

I could practically see Chasity standing in the front yard laughing as our kids ran through the grass. Two kids. Maybe even three if I could convince her. A dog. Probably something fluffy she'd pick out. Maybe even a cat, if she really insisted.

Family dinners. Movie nights. Lazy Sunday mornings where she stole all the blankets. A ring on her finger. A wedding. A future. All of it flashed through my mind in painful clarity.

Please God...

Don't take that away from us.

"Xavier!" Barry's hands grabbed my shoulders suddenly, shaking me hard. I blinked, snapping back into reality. "They found her!"

For a second my brain refused to understand the words. Then it hit me. "What?"

I rushed to the edge again and looked down at the cliff.

"How is she?" My voice cracked.

One of the men on the rope looked up from halfway down the cliff.

"Sir! She's badly hurt!"

My chest tightened painfully.

"Lots of cuts and bruises!" he shouted. "We don't know if anything is broken yet!"

My stomach twisted.

"But she has a pulse!" he added quickly. "It's faint… but it's there!"

The air rushed back into my lungs all at once. She was alive. Alive.

Above us the thundering roar of helicopter blades suddenly filled the night sky. The powerful sound vibrated through the trees as the aircraft hovered over the clearing. Spotlights flooded the forest with blinding white light. A rescue gurney was lowered slowly down the cliff.

I stood frozen as the team below carefully secured Chasity onto it. Every second felt like an hour. My hands clenched and unclenched helplessly. Then finally… The gurney began rising.

Slowly.

Slowly.

Out of the darkness. When she finally came into view my chest seized. Her body was limp. Her clothes were torn and soaked with blood and snow. Dark bruises already spread across her skin. My stomach was lurched violently.

"Let's go," Barry said firmly, turning me toward the path back to the cars. My legs moved automatically. I barely remembered running through the woods. I barely remember climbing into the SUV. Barely remember the frantic drive to the hospital. Everything felt unreal. Like I was watching someone else's life unfold.

When we arrived at the hospital, chaos exploded around us again. Doctors. Nurses. Bright fluorescent lights. They rushed Chasity straight through the emergency doors and disappeared down the hallway.

"Head trauma!" one of the doctors shouted.

"Possible internal bleeding!" The words stabbed into my chest like knives.

Nick and I weren't even allowed to follow. They pushed her straight into surgery. My body refused to sit. I paced the waiting room endlessly.

Back and forth.

Back and forth.

My hands shook so badly I had to shove them into my pockets. Chasity had to be okay. She still had her whole life ahead of her. She still had dreams. Plans. A future.

"Fuck Ryan," I muttered under my breath, rage burning through my chest. I hated that man with every fiber of my being. And worst of all… I failed her.

If I had been home…

If I hadn't left for Colorado…

None of this would have happened.

Nick stepped out of the waiting room to make phone calls. My mind was too scattered, too panicked to handle anything. Time dragged painfully. Minutes felt like hours. Eventually Nick came back.

"Joe and Bruce are on their way," he said quietly. "Once she's out of surgery, one of us will call her parents."

He guided me toward a chair. I sat. For maybe ten seconds. Then I stood up again. I couldn't sit still.

"She's going to be okay," Nick said.

I nodded. But I couldn't believe it. Not until I saw her.

Barry returned with two cups of steaming coffee. The rich smell filled the sterile hospital air as he handed one to each of us. I looked up at him.

"You should go home," I said quietly. My voice felt rough and fragile. "You've been on the clock for over twelve hours."

Barry shook his head slightly.

"I'm waiting for Landon to relieve me," he said. "Then I'll head out."

Time passed. More waiting. More pacing. More silence. Finally, the waiting room doors burst open. Joe and Bruce rushed in. Their faces pale with fear. We waited together. An eternity of anxious silence.

Then… The operating room doors opened. A doctor stepped out.

"Family?" he asked.

Joe stood immediately. Bruce placed a steady hand on his back.

"We're her family," Joe said.

The doctor nodded and led them into a consultation room. The door closed behind them. Another eternity passed. Finally, the door opened again. Joe walked out first. His face was wet with tears. My heart dropped into my stomach. Then he spoke.

"She's in the clear."

The words hit me like a wave.

"They stopped the bleeding," he continued, voice trembling. "They're moving her to the VIP suite now."

Bruce kissed Joe's temple and held him tightly.

"We can see her once she's settled."

My knees nearly gave out from relief.

* * * * *

Tristan leaned back in the office chair, lacing his fingers behind his head like he had all the time in the world.

"Please," he said dramatically, flipping his hands upward toward the camera, "take a moment to appreciate how awesome I am."

The smug grin on his face made my blood boil. I leaned forward on the couch, pinching my thumb and pointer finger together.

"I am this close to strangling you," I said through clenched teeth. "Your program failed us and nearly got Chasity killed."

Tristan clasped his hands together like he was praying and pushed his lips out in a ridiculous pout.

"I'm sorry," he said in a mock pitiful voice. "Please keep me alive. I still haven't found the love of my life yet."

I rolled my eyes so hard it hurt.

"Now tell me," I snapped, leaning forward, my heart already pounding again, "how the hell did he get access into my building when I specifically told all security not to let him in?"

Tristan pointed at me through the screen.

"That's the thing," he said.

"He didn't break in."

The room suddenly felt colder.

"He got access," Tristan continued slowly, "because technically… he lived there."

For a second my brain refused to process what he had just said. Then rage exploded through me. I shot to my feet so fast the coffee table rattled.

"How did that fucker live in my building without me knowing?!"

Nick grabbed my arm before I could start pacing holes into the floor.

"Whoa, sit down," he said firmly, pulling me back onto the couch. "Let Tristan explain."

My chest heaved as I dropped back down, every muscle in my body vibrating with anger. Tristan cleared his throat.

"Ryan bought one of the apartments," he said. "Under his fiancée's name."

The words hit like a punch to the gut. My hands slid up into my hair as the reality sank in.

"Fuck!" I shouted. The sound echoed through the office.

It was my building. My security. My systems. And somehow that bastard had been living right under my nose. I had practically handed him the access he needed to get to Chasity. Nick's hand tightened on my shoulder.

"Hey," he said quietly. "This is not your fault."

I shook my head violently.

"How could it not be?"

"How could you have known?" Nick countered. "We didn't even know who Ryan was until Florida. That was barely a few months ago.

My chest rose and fell heavily as I tried to breathe through the anger clawing up my throat. Tristan spoke again.

"I hacked into his computer," he said. "And I found something you need to see."

I looked up sharply.

"I already sent it to you."

A second later my iPad chimed.

"Two files," Tristan added. "Watch them."

Then the video call ended. The screen went black. My hands were trembling as I picked up the iPad. Two files. I tapped the first one. The screen flickered.

Then the camera footage from my own living room filled the display. My stomach twisted. The timestamp read earlier that evening.

"I'm going to change quickly then I'll be out for dinner," Chasity's voice echoed from the speakers.

My heart clenched. On the screen she walked toward the bedroom, her hair swinging slightly as she disappeared through the door.

Chris moved toward the front door a few seconds later. The moment he opened it… Everything exploded. Chris stumbled backward instantly, screaming as his hands flew to his eyes. Pepper spray.

"Kate!" he shouted blindly.

Kate burst out of the kitchen with her gun drawn. Ryan stood calmly in the foyer. Like he had every right to be there. The moment Kate saw him, she moved. Fast. She fired.

Ryan knocked the gun aside before the shot could land. The two of them collided in a blur of movement. Punches. Elbows. The dull thud of bodies hitting furniture. They crashed from the foyer into the living room.

Kate fought like hell. Every movement was precise. Every strike calculated. But Ryan was bigger. Stronger. Faster. Suddenly he grabbed a lamp from the side table. Before Kate could react…

CRASH.

The sound of glass shattering echoed through the speakers as the lamp slammed into her head. Kate collapsed instantly. Blood began spilling down her blonde hair, dripping onto the hardwood floor in dark red streaks. My stomach lurched.

"Jesus Christ…" Nick muttered beside me.

Ryan did not even hesitate. He pulled a handkerchief from his pocket and rushed into the kitchen. Chris was at the sink, desperately splashing water into his eyes. Ryan grabbed a fistful of his hair and yanked his head back violently. Chris struggled. Kicked. Tried to fight him off. But Ryan pressed the handkerchief over his nose and mouth. Within seconds Chris's body went limp. He crumpled to the ground. The room fell silent on the footage.

Then Ryan calmly walked toward the bedroom. My chest tightened painfully.

"How did Chasity not hear any of this?" I whispered hoarsely.

Then it hit me.

Hard.

"Fuck."

My hand slammed against the couch.

"She didn't hear it because Maggie was screaming at her on my phone."

Nick nodded slowly.

"That's why Maggie had the flight attendant steal my phone."

My jaw clenched so hard it hurt. Every piece had been planned. Every distraction. Every second. On the screen Ryan emerged from the bedroom. Chasity was limp in his arms.

My heart stopped.

Two chains dangled from his hand as he carried her across the living room floor. He stepped over Kate's unconscious body like she was nothing. Then he disappeared through the door. The footage ended. The screen went black.

The room was silent except for the sound of my breathing. Heavy. Uneven. My mind was spinning. Ryan had removed the necklace. The bracelet. The tracking devices. I wiped my face quickly.

"Then how the hell did Tristan track her?" I muttered.

Nick's voice pulled me back. "Breathe."

I blinked. I hadn't even realized tears had started falling. Nick nodded toward the iPad.

"I know what you're thinking," he said. "How did Tristan track Chasity when Ryan removed the jewelry?"

I nodded slowly.

Nick leaned back slightly.

"I gave her a hairclip," he admitted.

My head snapped toward him.

"A hairclip?"

"With a tracker inside it."

My chest tightened again.

"When?" I asked.

"New Year's Eve," Nick said. "At my parents' party."

He shrugged.

"I had a feeling."

The breath left my lungs in a rush. Relief crashed through my chest so suddenly it almost hurt.

"Thank God…"

More tears filled my eyes. Nicholas Warrington. Billionaire playboy. Ruthless businessman. My best friend. And the man who had just saved the love of my life. Nick wrapped an arm around my shoulders and pulled me close.

"Hey," he said quietly. "I got you. We're brothers."

I bit my fist as the tears finally spilled over.

"Thank you," I whispered.

For the first time since that nightmare began… I finally allowed myself to breathe.

Chapter 30

CHASITY

The first thing I heard was the sound. A steady, rhythmic beep… beep… beep…

It floated through the quiet room like a metronome, slow and constant. For a moment I thought I was dreaming. My body felt impossibly heavy, like I had been buried beneath layers of stone. Every muscle ached. My bones throbbed. Even breathing felt like work.

Then the smell reached me. Antiseptic. Clean sheets. Hospital.

My eyelids fluttered open. Bright white lights flooded my vision, forcing me to squint. My head pounded, and the ceiling above me seemed to spin for a moment before slowly coming into focus. White ceiling. White walls. Machines. The steady beep… beep… beep…

My throat felt dry and raw, like I hadn't had water in days. I shifted slightly. Instant regret. A sharp, stabbing pain exploded through my leg and radiated through my entire body. I gasped softly. A gentle voice spoke immediately.

"Easy."

I turned my head slowly. My mom sat beside the bed, gripping my hand so tightly it almost hurt. Her eyes were swollen and red like she had been crying for hours.

My dad stood on the other side of the bed; arms folded across his chest like he was trying to hold himself together. His jaw was tight, but his eyes were just red. Behind them stood half my family; my sister, my brother, two cousins, and a pair of aunts crowded near the door.

"Mom?" My voice came out scratchy and weak.

The moment she heard me speak; she broke down. Tears streamed down her face as she leaned forward, clutching my hand. "Oh, thank God."

My dad cleared his throat and leaned closer. "You're safe, sweetheart."

The words settled slowly in my mind.

Safe.

My brain struggled to piece together the last thing I remembered. The forest. The cold. Ryan's arm around my neck. The gun. The cliff. My stomach twisted.

"Ryan…" I whispered.

My dad's expression hardened. "He's gone."

Silence filled the room.

Not relief.

Not celebration.

Just quiet.

I closed my eyes for a moment and let out a slow breath. It was over.

Ten years. Ten years of fear, nightmares, and always looking over my shoulder. And now… it was finally over.

My aunt stepped closer to the bed. "The doctors said you're very lucky."

I blinked at her. "Lucky?"

"Just dehydration, exhaustion, and a broken leg from the fall," she explained softly.

"You scared the life out of us." Alexi wiped her eyes and stepped closer.

I managed to smile. "I scared myself too."

My mom squeezed my hand again.

"You're coming home with us to Montana," she said firmly.

I blinked. "Mom…"

"No arguments. You need real rest," my dad said gently. He softened a little. "And you're not doing that alone."

For once… I did not argue. I was too tired. And maybe… home was exactly what I needed.

* * * * *

Two weeks later, I stood in my childhood bedroom. Sunlight poured through the open window, warming the wooden floor beneath my feet. The scent of pine drifted inside with the cool mountain breeze. Outside, the mountains stretched across the horizon exactly the way they had when I was a little girl. Nothing here had changed.

Except me.

It had been two long weeks of not seeing Xavier in person, even though we texted all day long and talked every night before bed. It was not the same. No matter how many messages we exchanged or how long we stayed on the phone, there was still a distance I could feel. There was something missing that only his presence could fill.

Thankfully, my workplace was willing to give me a month of leave due to the physical and emotional impact that the kidnapping had on me. I did not argue. I needed the time, even if I did not fully understand how much yet.

I missed Xavier more than I expected. More than I wanted to admit. I could not wait to go back home and see him. To exist in the same space again without a screen or a call separating us.

He told me he was working on sorting out everything that happened with Ryan. He told me about everything. How the whole plan had been orchestrated. How calculated it had all been. And what his legal team was handling with the Weiss family.

It sounded exhausting.

Heavy.

It was complicated in ways that I did not fully understand but could feel the weight of. A part of me felt guilty, I was the one who brought Ryan to Xavier's doorstep. Ryan's chaos had followed me and spilled into Xavier's world. But at the same time, I felt something else too. There was a great deal of gratitude that I had Xavier and Nick in my corner.

Without them, I did not even want to think about what could have happened. I might not have been able to leave Montana. Ryan might have found a way to get me here.

But I was not going to dwell on it. I knew better than that. Dwelling on the what-ifs would only drag me into a spiral I would not be able to climb out of. I took a deep breath that was slow and intentional. I grounded myself in the present. I recentered and focused on what was real and what was in front of me. Then I repeated quiet affirmations to myself in a steady and deliberate voice. I let them push back against any lingering fears and thoughts that tried to pull me under.

My leg was still in a cast, resting carefully on a chair as I adjusted the sleeve of my sweater. A knock sounded on the door.

Justin poked his head inside. "Ready?"

"For what?" I looked at him.

He grinned. "The small get together, duh."

"Do I have to go?" I frowned.

"Yes."

An hour later, we were driving up a long gravel road carved into the side of a mountain. I stared out the window, confused.

"I thought this was just a small family gathering."

Alexi smirked beside me. "It is."

The car stopped. I stepped out carefully, balancing with my crutches. Then I looked up. My breath caught.

A massive ranch estate sat at the top of the hill. It was beautiful, built from dark timber and stone, with warm lights glowing through every window. The house overlooked acres of rolling land and the valley stretching far below. It looked like something out of a dream.

"Wait," I said slowly. I turned to my family. "Whose place is this?"

Justin simply gestured toward the house. "Let's get inside."

Still confused, I walked toward the front door slowly in my crutches. Justin opened before I even touched them.

And there he was.

Xavier.

My heart skipped.

He stood in the foyer, looking nervous and relieved all at the same time.

"Hi," he said softly.

I stared at him. "What are you doing here?"

He stepped closer.

"I've been waiting."

"For what?"

"For you to come home."

I looked around the house again.

"Whose ranch is this?"

He smiled. "It's yours."

"What?" My eyebrows shot up.

"I bought it," he said casually. "A few weeks ago."

I blinked. “You bought… a mountain ranch?”

“So, whenever you want to come home…” He nodded and gestured toward the mountains outside. “You’ll always have a place.”

My chest tightened. “You didn’t have to do that.”

“I know.”

He reached into his pocket. “But there’s something I need to do.”

My heart started beating faster. Xavier slowly lowered himself onto one knee. My hands flew to my mouth.

“This past year,” he said quietly, “we’ve been through a lot. New York. Florida. And what just happened.”

His eyes softened. “When I thought I might lose you… I realized something.”

He opened a small velvet box. A diamond ring sparkled inside.

“I don’t know what tomorrow brings,” he said. “But I know one thing. I want every tomorrow I have, to be with you.”

Tears filled my eyes.

“Will you marry me?”

My heart exploded with love and happiness. The feeling was so overwhelming that it almost felt impossible to contain. It filled my chest and rushed through me. I was left breathless in the most beautiful way. I loved Xavier with all my heart. There was no hesitation in it. No doubt. It was just a steady and undeniable truth that had grown stronger with every moment we had shared. He was the one I wanted to spend the rest of my life with. The one I chose over and over again without any question.

He loved me and protected me in every way possible. In every way that he knew how to. He stepped up when he did not have to. He came through for me when it would have been easier to simply walk away. He could have left me and everything that came with me behind. But he did not. He could have wiped his hands clean of me and my baggage. He could have chosen a simpler path and a much less complicated life. But he stayed. He chose me. And I loved this man. This man who was kneeling in front of me. In front of our families and friends and asking me to be his wife.

I nodded before he even finished. “Yes!”

He slipped the ring onto my finger and stood. I wrapped my arms around him carefully, mindful of my leg.

“I love you,” I whispered.

"I love you too." Then he kissed me. And outside the front doors, our families burst into cheers.

Everyone spent the evening indulging in food and drinks. It was the kind of lively and overlapping energy that only came when families gathered for something meaningful. Laughter carried easily through the space. Conversations blended into one another as people moved from table to table, introducing themselves, reconnecting, and sharing stories.

Both sides of the family were getting to know each other, though the contrast was impossible to miss. Xavier's family was much smaller with just his mother, sister, brother-in-law, and niece in addition to Nick, his parents, and Bruce and Joe. While my family filled the place with aunts, uncles, cousins, and extended relatives. Everyone's voices were layered and animated. It could have been overwhelming, but my family welcomed them with open arms, pulled them in without hesitation, and made space for them like they had always been there.

I watched as my parents sat with his mother. They were already deep in conversation. My parents were explaining the traditional wedding ceremony with animated gestures and knowing smiles. I shook my head softly as a small laugh slipped out under my breath. They were getting way ahead of themselves. Xavier had just proposed. The moment still felt fresh and unreal in the best way possible. And here they were, already talking about ceremonies and traditions. The wedding was not going to be anytime soon. I still had to wait for my leg to recover because there was no way I was walking down the aisle in a cast.

Even as the future began to take shape around me in everyone else's conversations, I stayed grounded in the present. I was going to let myself fully feel this moment before rushing into the next.

Epilogue

CHASITY

The mountain air was crisp that morning. I could smell pine, wild grass, and the faint sweetness of the wildflowers growing along the hillside. Sunlight spilled across the valley below like liquid gold, and a soft breeze drifted through the tall trees surrounding the ranch.

Everything felt calm.

Peaceful.

The kind of peace I had spent years thinking I would never feel again. I stood at the top of the hill overlooking the ceremony setup and took a slow breath, letting the cool air fill my lungs.

Rows of wooden chairs stretched across the open meadow below. White and pale blue ribbons fluttered gently from the backs of each chair, dancing softly in the wind. At the end of the aisle stood a beautiful wooden arch covered in greenery, white roses, and small wildflowers gathered from the mountains surrounding the ranch.

Beyond the arch, the entire valley opened like a painting. Mountains layered one behind another in shades of deep blue and green. The sky above was perfectly clear. It was the most beautiful place I had ever seen. And today… I am getting married here.

"Chasity." My mom's voice pulled me from my thoughts.

I turned around slowly.

She stood in the doorway of the ranch house with tears already forming in her eyes.

"You look beautiful."

I smiled nervously and glanced down at the dress.

The fabric was soft ivory lace that flowed gently to the ground, light enough to move with the mountain breeze. The sleeves were delicate and sheer, with tiny, embroidered flowers climbing from my wrists to my shoulders.

My cast had been removed weeks ago, but my leg still felt a little stiff. Still… I had insisted on walking down the aisle myself. I had already lost too many moments in my life. I wasn't losing this one.

My sister stepped behind me and adjusted the veil resting against my hair.

"You ready?" she asked softly.

I swallowed and nodded. "I think so."

The music began drifting across the meadow. Soft piano. The guests quieted instantly. Through the open windows I could hear the murmur of voices settling into silence, the rustle of dresses and suits as everyone stood.

My heart started beating faster.

My dad walked over and offered me his arm. "Ready, sweetheart?"

I slipped my hand through his arm. Together we stepped out onto the path leading toward the aisle. The moment we turned the corner; the entire gathering came into view.

Friends.

Family.

People who had supported me through the darkest years of my life. Joe and Bruce sat in the front row, both smiling proudly. Nick stood near the arch beside the officiant, already grinning like he knew he was about to tease Xavier later. And then… I saw him.

Xavier stood beneath the arch.

The moment our eyes met, everything else faded away. The crowd. The mountains. The music.

All I could see was him.

His dark suit fit him perfectly, but his expression was what made my heart melt. His eyes were soft and bright, filled with a kind of happiness that made my chest ache. Like he couldn't quite believe this moment was real either.

The breeze lifted my veil as we began walking down the aisle. Each step felt surreal. I could hear the soft crunch of grass beneath my shoes, feel my father's steady arm supporting me, smell the fresh flowers lining the aisle. The sunlight warmed my shoulders. By the time we reached the front, my eyes were already full of tears.

My dad squeezed my hand gently.

"You take care of her," he told Xavier.

Xavier nodded immediately. "With my life."

My dad patted my hand and stepped back. Xavier reached for my hands. The warmth of his fingers wrapped around mine instantly, grounding me.

"You look incredible," he whispered.

I laughed softly through my tears. "So do you."

The officiant began speaking, but the words felt distant. All I could focus on was Xavier. The way his thumbs gently brushed over my knuckles. The way his eyes never left mine. His voice trembled slightly when it was time for his vows.

"Chasity," he began softly. "I spent years building businesses, chasing success, trying to control every outcome in life."

A small smile touched his lips.

"But loving you taught me something different. You taught me that the most important things in life can't be controlled. They can only be cherished."

His voice grew thicker.

"I promise to protect you, to support you, to stand beside you no matter what life throws at us. I promise to build a life with you filled with laughter, adventure, and as many quiet mornings together as we can get."

He took a small breath.

"And I promise that no matter where we are in the world… Home will always be wherever you are."

Tears slipped down my cheeks. When it was my turn, my voice trembled too.

"Xavier… you came into my life at a time when I didn't think I deserved happiness anymore."

My fingers tightened around his fingers.

"You didn't just love me. You believed in me. You helped me find myself again."

The wind stirred gently around us.

"And I promise to love you, support you, and walk beside you for every chapter of our lives. Even the messy ones."

He laughed softly at that. The officiant smiled warmly.

"By the power vested in me… You may kiss the bride."

Xavier did not hesitate. He pulled me gently toward him and kissed me. The crowd erupted into cheers and applause. Nick whistled loudly. I laughed against Xavier's lips. When we finally pulled apart, he rested his forehead against mine.

"Mrs. Sterling," he whispered.

The mountains stretched endlessly behind us as the wind carried the sound of laughter and celebration across the valley. And for the first time in my life… My future felt completely, beautifully open.

* * * * *

XAVIER

The groom's suite was quiet but not silent. There was a low hum of movement. Shoes on the hardwood, the faint clink of cufflinks being clasped onto cuffs, and the soft rustle of fabric as I adjusted my jacket for what felt like the tenth time. The mirror in front of me reflected a man I barely recognized. Not because I looked different, but because of what this moment meant.

Today, I was getting married to Chasity.

I exhaled slowly while straightening my tie. I was trying to steady the energy building in my chest. I had stood in boardrooms with billions on the line. Negotiated deals that could make or break entire companies. None of that compared to this. None of that had ever made my hands feel like this… where they were slightly unsteady. Like everything I was holding onto mattered more than anything I had ever touched before.

"You're going to wear a hole in that floor if you keep pacing like that."

Nick's voice cut through my thoughts. He was as casual as ever. I glanced over at him. He was leaning against the wall with that same knowing grin he always had when he thought something was entertaining.

"I'm not pacing," I muttered.

"You are," he said immediately. "And it's very entertaining. Xavier Sterling. Self-made billionaire. CEO and co-founder of Sterling and Co have been reduced to a nervous groom. I should record this for blackmail."

I let out a short breath, somewhere between a laugh and a sigh. "Whatever."

He pushed off the wall and walked over. A hand clapped on my shoulder. "Relax. Chasity won't run."

I shook my head slightly. "I'll catch her if she does."

Then we both laughed. I knew that Chasity loved me as much as I loved her. No one was running from our big day.

The door opened softly behind us, and I turned to see my mother step inside. The moment she saw me, her expression changed. She softened instantly, and her eyes were already shining.

"You look just like your father," she said. Her voice was gentle like she was holding something fragile.

I felt something shift in my chest at that.

She stepped closer and reached up to adjust my tie, despite it not needing any adjustments. "He would be so proud of you," she added quietly.

I swallowed; the weight of her words settled in deeper than I expected. "I hope so."

She smiled as her hand lingering for just a moment before dropping. "I know so."

There was a brief pause before she added softly, "She's a good woman."

"I know," I said immediately.

"And she loves you."

That one… I felt.

I nodded. "I know."

My mother smiled again, and this time was with something more certain behind it. "Then you're ready."

The music started not long after.

It drifted in from outside. The piano notes were carried by the breeze. The sound settled over everything and quieted the room without needing to demand it. Nick gave my shoulder one last squeeze before heading out ahead of me, and I followed.

When I reached the front and took my place beneath the arch, the world felt… still.

Beautiful.

But incomplete.

I barely noticed the guests, the mountains, and the endless stretch of sky behind me. It was all there, of course I knew it was, but none of it held my attention.

Because I was waiting.

And then…

She appeared.

The moment she turned the corner with her father, everything else disappeared.

Completely.

The sound faded.

The movement.

The world.

It was just her and me.

Chasity.

Walking toward me in that dress. The sunlight caught in her veil and the soft breeze moved around her like the world itself had slowed down just to let her pass through it. My chest tightened so suddenly I had to remind myself to breathe.

She was… unreal.

Not in the way people usually meant it. Not perfect. Not untouchable.

Real.

Mine.

Every step she took felt like it was pulling something in me closer to the surface, something I did not even try to control. My throat tightened. My vision blurred slightly. And I honestly did not care. I did not care who saw it.

Because all I could think was…

She was here.

She was really here.

By the time she reached me, I was already gone. Whatever version of me existed before this moment, before her, it did not matter anymore.

Because the only thing that mattered now…

Was that she chose me.

And I would spend the rest of my life proving that I deserved her.

Happily Ever After

About the Author

Uhn Muas lives in the Midwest with her husband and children. She spends her days caring for her family and home then her evenings are immersed in contemporary romance novels. Her nights are filled with dreaming of stories that stretched beyond the edges of human imagination.

Growing up, Uhn lost herself in books like *Harry Potter* and *The Lion, the Witch, and the Wardrobe.* Getting lost in books were the only vacations she was able to take. As the child of Hmong refugee parents, she was also surrounded by traditional stories such as Ntxawm and Nujnpliab, Ntxawm and Nraug Sivnab, and Zab.

In her free time, she enjoys binge watching Netflix series and trying out new burger joints. And of course, taking naps during the day to dream of faraway lands and magical beings.

Coming Soon...

THE CONTRACT

LUCY

I stared at the pregnancy test in my hand. The cheap plastic felt cold and smooth against my fingers, too light for something that suddenly felt so heavy. No matter how many times I squeezed my eyes shut and opened them again, the result never changed. The word positive glared up at me from the tiny screen like it was mocking me. I took a shaky breath and looked again, hoping the letters might somehow rearrange themselves if I blinked hard enough. They did not.

This was not the first test I had taken. It was already the third. All three of them had shown the exact same result. The first one had made my stomach drop. The second one had made my hands start shaking. The third one just made my chest feel hollow, like someone had scooped something out of me.

The faint chemical smell of the bathroom cleaner still clung to my fingers, mixing with the sterile plastic scent of the test. My heart pounded so loudly in my ears that it drowned out the quiet hum of the refrigerator down the hall.

It had to be a nightmare. What was I going to do? The question echoed in my head like a voice bouncing off empty walls. My mouth had gone dry, and when I swallowed it felt thick and uncomfortable, like I was trying to force down a lump of sand. This was not supposed to happen. It was not supposed to be like this. It was supposed to be clean and simple. Go in, do my job, and get out. No complications. No loose ends. No life-altering consequences growing quietly inside my body.

But reality did not care about plans. I dropped the pregnancy test onto the couch beside me. The small plastic stick landed with a soft, hollow tap against the fabric cushion. I leaned back slowly until my head rested against the back of the couch and stared up at the ceiling. The white paint looked dull under the yellowish glow of the living room lamp. A faint crack ran across one corner like a crooked line, something I had noticed a hundred times before but never really looked at until now.

A long sigh escaped my chest before I could stop it. My lungs felt tight, like the air in the room had suddenly gotten heavier. My palms were damp, and I wiped them against my jeans, feeling the rough denim scrape against my skin. My stomach twisted with a strange mix of fear and disbelief.

It was going to be okay. I repeated the thought in my head like a fragile promise. I was going to figure it out. I had to. The quiet house suddenly felt too still, the silence pressing around me. Somewhere outside, a car drove past and the distant sound of tires on pavement drifted through the window.

Financially, I was in a better position than I had been two years ago. I clung to that thought like a lifeline. I have more savings now. A more stable job. I had survived worse things than this in the past.

My hand drifted down unconsciously to rest against my stomach. “I can do it,” I whispered into the empty room.

www.ingramcontent.com/pod-product-compliance
Lightning Source LLC
LaVergne TN
LVHW040223110826
845146LV00004B/1258

* 9 7 9 8 9 9 5 2 8 3 4 3 0 *